FROM THE
NANCY DREW FILES

THE CASE: Nancy pursues a murderer down a trail of jealousy, greed, and deceit.

CONTACT: Searching for a near-extinct insect, Barb Sommers never imagined what she'd actually dig up.

SUSPECTS: D. J. Divott—He claimed to be Tom Haines's best friend, but when they fell for the same girl, he might have turned into his worst enemy.

Congressman Walt Winchester—A politician with plenty to hide, he'd resort to the dirtiest of tricks to keep his career on track.

Scott Winchester—The Congressman's rich, arrogant son, he may be leading a secret life . . . with a secret motive for murder!

COMPLICATIONS: The one murder suspect who may know the truth about Tom Haines's past and the reasons for his death refuses to talk to Nancy . . . even though he could clear his own name.

Books in The Nancy Drew Files® Series

Available from ARCHWAY Paperbacks

The Nancy-Drew Files™

Case 98
Island of Secrets
Carolyn Keene

AN ARCHWAY PAPERBACK
Published by POCKET BOOKS
New York London Toronto Sydney Tokyo Singapore

AN ARCHWAY PAPERBACK *Original*

An Archway Paperback published by
POCKET BOOKS, a division of Simon & Schuster Inc.
1230 Avenue of the Americas, New York, NY 10020

Copyright © 1994 by Simon & Schuster Inc.
Produced by Mega-Books of New York, Inc.

All rights reserved, including the right to reproduce
this book or portions thereof in any form whatsoever.
For information address Pocket Books, 1230 Avenue
of the Americas, New York, NY 10020

ISBN: 0-671-79490-6

First Archway Paperback printing August 1994

10 9 8 7 6 5 4 3 2 1

NANCY DREW, AN ARCHWAY PAPERBACK and colophon
are registered trademarks of Simon & Schuster Inc.

THE NANCY DREW FILES is a trademark of
Simon & Schuster Inc.

Cover art by Cliff Miller

Printed in the U.S.A.

IL 6+

Island of Secrets

Chapter

One

NANCY DREW LEANED against the rail of the ferryboat, shading her eyes as she gazed at the dark smudge on the horizon she knew was Block Island. When Hannah Gruen, the Drews' gray-haired housekeeper, came to her side, Nancy turned with a smile. "Isn't it great, Hannah? Two whole weeks of vacation!"

"It's about time, too," Hannah replied, her hazel eyes twinkling. "You work too hard on your detective cases. You deserve a rest."

"I'm so glad you came with me," Nancy said, giving Hannah a hug. "We'll have a terrific time."

Hannah nodded, then peeked back toward the mainland. The ferry had just cleared the Point Judith breakwater, leaving the little fishing town of Galilee behind. "I wish your father could have

1

come with us. He needs a vacation, too. Do you think he'll manage all right on his own?"

Nancy laughed. "You left enough food in the refrigerator to feed not only him, but the judge and jury, too. Besides, he's so involved in his trial he probably won't notice we're gone."

To take Hannah's mind off her worries, Nancy pulled out a map of Block Island from her purse. "Can you believe how small the island is?"

Hannah put on the reading glasses that hung from a chain around her neck. "Why, it's only seven miles long."

"And only about three and a half across at the widest point. This huge bay called Great Salt Pond on the west side almost cuts it in half."

Hannah studied the map. "I'd say the island's shaped something like a pork chop."

Nancy chuckled. "Our cottage is in Old Harbor, the only town on the east coast. But there are lots of things to see all over the island. Aunt Eloise said we should rent mopeds to get around easier."

"Me? On a moped?" Hannah half-cried.

"It's easy," Nancy replied. "I'll teach you."

"We'll see." Hannah shivered slightly and pulled her blue cotton cardigan closed across her chest. "This wind is rather strong. Let's go inside."

"I'll join you in a moment," Nancy said. She was enjoying the salt air and the sparkling blue sea.

As Hannah made her way across the crowded deck, Nancy looked around. Other passengers were happily chatting on this sunny Sunday morning in August.

Beside her, a pretty girl of about twelve leaned eagerly over the rail, her long dark hair blowing in the breeze. She saw Nancy looking at her and smiled.

"I love watching the waves," the girl confided. "We don't have an ocean in Library, Pennsylvania."

"We don't have one in River Heights, Illinois, either," Nancy admitted, introducing herself.

"I'm Ashley Hanna," the girl said. "My family and I come to the island every summer. My uncle runs a marina in Great Salt Pond. I get to help him on the docks and stuff. It's great."

Just then a woman's voice called out, "Ashley!" and the girl turned to leave. "I've got to go," she said over her shoulder. "Maybe I'll see you around."

Nancy decided to find Hannah in the enclosed part of the ferry. Once inside, she looked around for her friend.

She smiled when she spotted Hannah headed for a white-haired woman sitting under one of the big windows. The woman had pieces of patchwork quilting spread over her lap. Hannah was an enthusiastic quilter, and the Drew home was full of her handiwork.

Nancy came up to the two women just as

3

Hannah was saying, "I couldn't help noticing your quilting. That's the Double Wedding Ring design, isn't it?"

The older woman raised her head. Her face was softly lined and her brown eyes were lively. "Why, yes, it is. Do you quilt, too?"

Hannah nodded. "I brought my Sunshine and Shadows pattern with me." She opened her tote bag and took out one of the gaily colored quilt squares.

"Oh, how lovely," the lady said, smoothing the fabric with gentle fingers. "I'm Sarah Windsor, and I own the Crazy for Crafts shop on Block. I'm making this for my daughter. She's getting married in the fall, so I had to make the Double Wedding Ring for her."

Hannah introduced herself and Nancy, then sat down next to Sarah. Nancy knew Hannah would be happily involved for the rest of the trip, so she excused herself, saying she wanted to explore.

Out on deck she slowly made her way toward the stern where she could peer down on the ferry's lower level, full of cars and trucks parked bumper to bumper, and bikes and luggage squeezed in on the sides. Then she climbed the steps to the top deck and found a spot at the railing. For a while, she leaned into the warm breeze and watched the sailboats skim across the water. Then she noticed the tall, slender girl with honey-blond hair standing next to her. She wore a T-shirt that said, Have You Hugged a Bug Lately?

The girl turned to Nancy. "Have you been to Block before?" she asked amiably.

Nancy smiled into her warm blue eyes. "No, but I'm really looking forward to it."

"Are you traveling alone?" the girl asked.

"I'm with a friend," Nancy answered. "Is this your first visit to Block, too?"

The girl shook her head. "No, I've been working there all summer with the Nature Conservancy. I'm in graduate school, working on my thesis."

"What are you studying?" Nancy asked.

The girl made a face. "Promise you won't say 'icky' or 'yuck'?"

"Promise," Nancy said, her curiosity aroused.

"I'm studying an extremely rare insect, the American burying beetle. It used to be found in thirty-two states, but now it's almost extinct. There are only a few hundred left in the world and Block Island has one of the two surviving colonies."

"Really?" Nancy said, intrigued. "Why is the beetle so rare?"

The girl frowned. "That's what we're trying to pin down. We think it's partly because of pesticides."

"So the work you're doing might save the beetles from extinction?" Nancy asked.

"We *hope* so." After a moment the girl's frown

5

faded and she held out her hand to Nancy. "I'm Barb Sommers. It's nice to meet someone who isn't grossed out by bugs."

"I'm Nancy Drew." She shook Barb's hand. "I think the beetles sound fascinating. What do they look like?"

Barb's face lit up. "They're beautiful! Would you like to see for yourself? I'm going over to the Lewis-Dickens farm this afternoon—it's a nature preserve where the main colony is found. You could come with me if you'd like."

"I'd love to," Nancy said.

"Where are you staying?"

Nancy gave her the address of the cottage.

"We're just around the corner from you! My roommate and I share the second floor of a house." She told Nancy how to find it. "How did you hear about Block? Are you from around here?"

"No, River Heights, near Chicago," Nancy said. "We flew out yesterday and stayed with my aunt in New York, then drove up to Rhode Island this morning. My aunt Eloise had rented the cottage, but a big work assignment came up so she called and offered it to us."

"You'll love Block," Barb said. "I'll introduce you to the crowd I hang out with. Some of the guys are native Islanders."

"I'd like to meet them," Nancy said, her thoughts already turning to her boyfriend, Ned Nickerson. She missed him and wished he'd been able to come with her, but Ned had already made plans for a canoe trip when Nancy's aunt had called a few days ago. Fortunately, her best friends, Bess Marvin and George Fayne, planned to join her and Hannah at the end of the week.

"The gang usually hangs out at a place called the Spotted Dog," Barb continued. For the next hour she talked about beetles, her friends, and the island itself. By the time the ferry docked, Nancy felt as if she knew Block well.

When Nancy and Hannah arrived on the pier, they were met by the agent who'd rented the cottage to Nancy's aunt Eloise. Nancy waved goodbye to Barb as the man ushered them into the backseat of his jeep, then drove a short distance through streets filled with people, bicycles, mopeds, and cars. Their cottage turned out to be a charming Victorian with white gingerbread trim and rosebushes, set on a hill above the town. The rooms were bright with cheerful yellow curtains and comfortable furniture. Hannah was pleased with the spotless kitchen and Nancy loved the porch overlooking the town and ocean beyond.

As soon as they unpacked, they walked down the hill to a sandwich shop for a late lunch. Afterward, Hannah returned to the cottage for a nap and Nancy set out for Barb's. The small saltbox with red shutters proved easy to find. Nancy climbed up the outside wooden staircase to the second floor apartment and knocked on the door. It was opened by a pretty, dark-haired girl in a waitress uniform.

"Hi, I'm Angelina Cassetti," she said in a soft voice. "You must be Nancy. Barb will be ready in a sec. Come on in."

Nancy stepped into a large room with gleaming oak floors. Futons and oversize pillows in soft hues took the place of furniture, and glossy green plants hung in the windows. A low table, like those Nancy had seen in Japanese restaurants, was placed opposite a tiny kitchenette.

"What a nice place," Nancy said.

"Thank you." Angelina scrutinized everything as if seeing it through a stranger's eyes. "The landlady reduced our rent after we refinished the floor and painted. And Barb has a friend whose father owns an import-export store so we got everything at a discount. I have to save most of what I make as a waitress for college expenses, and Barb's grant isn't very large—"

"So we put hard work together with Angie's decorating genius and ended up with this," Barb interrupted, coming out of the bedroom.

"Well, it looks great," Nancy said, smiling at Angie. "You're really talented."

"Oh, well . . ." Angie blushed.

"Let's get going," Barb said, grabbing a knapsack. "I can't wait to see how my bugs made out while I was off-island. Angie's letting you borrow her moped and helmet."

"Thanks, Angie," Nancy said.

"No problem. I can walk. The place I work—the Bell Buoy—is just down the hill from here." Angie glanced at her watch. "Whoops, I'm late. Say hello to the little guys for me."

In ten minutes Nancy was sitting on Angie's moped, following Barb along the hilly, winding roads toward the southwest corner of the island. The sea breeze caressed her face and lifted her strawberry blond hair off her shoulders. From somewhere nearby she caught sweet whiffs of honeysuckle. Soon Barb slowed down and turned into a side lane. A short while later they stopped at the edge of a field.

"See that rock wall over there?" Barb slung her knapsack on her back and pointed. "The Conservancy set up a trap line along it and I'm going to check it. The beetles are mainly nocturnal, so I can't *promise* we'll see one."

Nancy followed Barb across the grassy field. "Why are they called burying beetles?"

"Because they bury their food, then lay eggs in a nest and feed the babies from the food they've stored. They're one of few insects that care for their young once they hatch—the way birds do."

As they walked, Nancy noticed wild blackberry and bayberry bushes skirting the field. In the distance she could just make out the dark blue Atlantic Ocean.

They reached the rock wall and Barb stooped

down. "Here we are." She removed a flat piece of wood propped up by a stick that formed a miniature roof over a hole in the ground.

Nancy knelt beside her. A large glass jar was buried up to its neck in the soil. Inside, on the bottom, was a small baby-food jar with a screen covering the opening. She caught a whiff of a strong odor and pulled back. "Wheee-oouu."

"That's the bait in the little jar." Barb grinned. "The beetles think it smells delicious. They're drawn to it and fall into the large jar. They can't climb back up the smooth sides, so they're caught for the night. In the morning we count them and let them go. Someone's done the morning count already, but once in a while we get a stray."

They moved on to the next trap and Barb let out a whoop when she looked inside. "You're in luck, Nancy! This little guy is out past his bedtime!" Barb reached into the jar, carefully removed the insect, and held it out on her open palm.

The beetle was about two inches long and glossy black, with brilliant orange spots. It waved its feelers as if to test the air, then flew off with a loud whirring noise.

"Wow," Nancy said. "I feel privileged."

Barb nodded. "I know what you mean. You've just seen one of the world's endangered species."

Nancy watched as Barb checked the rest of the trap line. When she was finished, Barb said,

"Let's walk back by a different route. There's a great view from the top of that hill over there."

They headed up to another stone wall. On the far side of it was a dirt drive that led to a pond bordered by a clump of pine trees. Nancy was startled by what she thought was a pheasant in the tangled underbrush. Trying to get a better look, she crept closer. The bird flew off, and it was then she noticed something odd about the ground where the bird had been hiding behind the bushes. The earth was slightly mounded, and the grass on top of it was dry and brown, dead looking.

"Barb," Nancy called. "There's something strange here."

Barb hurried over and surveyed the mound that covered an area almost seven feet long and four feet wide. "I hope no one has been digging here for beetles," she said, pulling a collapsible shovel from her knapsack and snapping it open.

She removed several shovelfuls of dirt, then gasped and stepped back. Something was buried there. Something an ugly gray color.

Nancy took the shovel from her and scooped away more earth.

"No! Stop!" Barb cried, grabbing Nancy's arm.

"We have to see what it is," Nancy said grimly, though she had already guessed. Lifting a final shovelful of soil, Nancy no longer had any doubts.

A human hand lay exposed in the dirt.

11

Chapter

Two

BARB STARED IN HORROR. "It's a body. . . ."

"We'd better call the police," Nancy said.

"There's a ph-phone at the convenience store down the . . ." Barb began to point, then dropped her arm and silently stared at Nancy.

"It's okay." Nancy led Barb away from the makeshift grave. "Take a deep breath. . . . Good, now let it out." Trying to calm Barb distracted Nancy from the nausea that was rising from her stomach. Color slowly returned to Barb's face.

"I'll go call the police. Are you coming?"

"I'd better stay here." Nancy kept her eyes averted from the grisly sight.

"I'll be back as soon as I can," Barb cried, racing across the field toward the mopeds.

While she waited, Nancy searched the immediate area. She and Barb had left a trail of flattened meadow grass, but there was no other sign of intrusion. She walked to the dirt driveway. As she passed the shallow pond, the glint of something metallic in the water caught her eye. The object was a few feet from shore, mostly covered with duckweed. She was tempted to find a stick and drag it out, but knew that if it turned out to be related to the case she should leave it for the police.

Soon she heard the wail of an approaching siren and minutes later a police cruiser sped toward her. A young, sandy-haired officer stopped the car and stepped out. "Are you Miss Drew?" he asked. "Can you show me what you found?"

"It's behind those bushes," Nancy said, leading the way. Just as they reached the grave site more police cars arrived. Nancy moved out of the way while they photographed and put tape up around the potential crime scene. Soon, Barb returned, followed by a doctor, who was there to certify the death.

Nancy put an arm around Barb to steady her as the officers began to remove the rest of the soil covering the body. When the head was revealed, Nancy heard shocked exclamations. She and Barb were standing too far away to see into the grave very well.

Next the young officer came over to question them, flipping his notebook open in an attempt to appear official and calm. Still, Nancy noticed

13

that his hands shook and his freckles stood out in sharp contrast to his ashen face.

Before he could begin his questions Barb burst out, "Who is it?"

The officer hesitated, glanced back at the corpse, then said, "It's not official until the body is formally identified."

"It's someone we know, isn't it?" Barb pressed.

"Well, it looks like Tom Haines." The officer cleared his throat, then swallowed hard.

"Tom Haines?" Barb whispered. "It can't be!"

Before Nancy could stop her, Barb ran to the grave site. She stared at the body for a moment, then spun around and stumbled away, sobbing.

Nancy led Barb over to the stone wall and helped her to sit. It was some minutes before Barb was able to speak.

"It's just so—unreal," she said, shuddering.

"He was a friend of yours?" Nancy asked.

"Yes, he's one of our gang. I even dated him a few times. . . ." She burst into tears again.

The young officer waited at a distance until Barb was calm enough to talk, then identified himself as Sgt. Jim Hathaway. He started by writing down their names. Nancy answered most of his questions, describing how they'd found the body.

When the sergeant finished and snapped his notebook shut, Nancy said, "I noticed something you might want to check out. There's a metal object in the pond."

He seemed skeptical, but he agreed to check it out. Nancy led him and Barb to the edge of the water. After a brief search, she found it and pointed it out.

Squinting into the glare off the water, he said, "It looks like a hammer. You didn't touch it, did you?"

"No. I knew it could turn out to be important," Nancy said.

"That was smart. Most people would have fished it out right away."

"Well, I've had some detective experience," Nancy said. "I know not to disturb evidence."

"Detective experience?" Hathaway raised an eyebrow. "A pretty girl like you?"

Nancy told him about a few of the cases she'd solved. She could see that he was impressed.

Barb, too, acted respectful, saying, "If you're a detective, maybe you could find out how Tom—"

"I'm sure Sergeant Hathaway and the others can handle the investigation," Nancy replied.

"Why don't you call me Jim?" Hathaway said. "After all, we're colleagues in a way, and it seems that you have more experience than I do when it comes to murder. Probably more than the senior officers on the force. A murder has never happened on Block, not in my memory."

"So you *do* think it's murder?" Nancy asked.

"What else could it be?" Jim said. "Tom was only twenty-four, a big guy, healthy as a horse."

15

"You knew him well?" Nancy asked.

"It's a small island, especially once the tourists leave. Only about eight hundred of us live here year-round. Tom and I grew up together, but he was several years ahead of me in school. He was something of a troublemaker, to be honest."

"That's not fair!" Barb said. "He had a rough life, but I know a lot of guys like him where I come from, in South Boston. And how can you talk about him that way? He's dead!" Barb burst into tears and ran toward the mopeds.

"Let her go," Jim told Nancy. "She needs time. But she's making a mistake, trying to defend Tom. The guy was bad news."

"What do you mean?" Nancy asked.

"He was always trying to make a buck, and he didn't care how he got it. His junior year in high school, he ran a gambling ring. It only lasted until he was caught with a marked deck of cards, but that was just peanuts compared to what I heard he did later. And I *know* he was into something big this summer."

"What?" Nancy asked.

"I'm not sure, but it definitely wasn't honest," Jim said. "He was flashing a lot of money around, talking about buying his own boat, and he hadn't worked in almost two months. Even a used boat costs plenty these days, so he must have had something big going."

A police lieutenant came over to them. Jim introduced Nancy, then showed him the hammer. They dragged it from the pond with a long stick and dropped it into a plastic evidence bag.

"The chief wants you to head back to the station," the lieutenant said. "Get this ready to send off to the lab, then start on your report."

"Yes, sir," Jim said as he strode away. He turned to Nancy. "Thanks for your help, Miss Drew."

"Nancy, please," she said.

He smiled for the first time, a boyish grin. "Could you come down to headquarters in a little while? I'll type up the statements for you and Barb to sign."

"Sure," Nancy said. "We'll meet you there."

Barb was waiting for her by the mopeds, her eyes puffy and red from weeping. When Nancy told her about Jim's request, Barb nodded, then mounted her bike and silently led the way back to the main road, turning north toward Great Salt Pond.

They stopped for a soda at the convenience store where Barb had phoned the police. This seemed to calm down Barb. Then they rode to the police station, which was located minutes from the center of Old Harbor.

As Nancy and Barb walked in, they were greeted by the dispatcher in her small office to the right of the door. "You can wait for Sergeant Hathaway in there," the woman told them, pointing to the main room. The phone rang and she snatched it up. "No, I can't comment about a murder," she told the caller, annoyed. "The chief will be making an official statement later today." She hung up and the phone rang again. Shaking her head, she repeated the same thing to the next caller.

Several people were sitting in the main room, and through an open door, Nancy could see into the garage where the patrol cars were parked.

"Do you know anything about the murder?" a short, bald man with a notebook asked Nancy.

"No," she replied.

The man hurried over to a young couple who had just come in and questioned them eagerly. More and more people arrived. Nancy was relieved when Jim appeared and led them into a small office crowded with three desks. Barb had remained very quiet the whole time. After Jim typed her statement into the computer, she signed the printout, checked to be sure Nancy knew the way home, then quickly left.

By the time Nancy had signed her own statement, the small police station was abuzz with excitement. At least a dozen people milled around, exchanging rumors about the murder.

"Can I buy you a cup of coffee?" Jim offered, glancing at his watch. "I'm due for a short break."

"I'd love it," Nancy answered.

He was leading her to the door when a tall, distinguished man with iron gray hair called out,

"Sergeant Hathaway, could I see you for a moment?"

They stopped and turned around. "Certainly, Congressman," Jim said with respect. "What can I do for you?"

The man strode toward them, followed by a very blond, very handsome young man. "What in blazes is going on here?" the older man asked with an accent that sounded vaguely Western. "We came to file a complaint against trespassers on our property and found this place busy as a barn at milking time."

Jim lowered his voice. "A body was found earlier this afternoon, sir. In fact, this young lady was one of the people who reported it. Nancy Drew, this is State Congressman Walt Winchester and his son, Scott. The Winchesters are building a house on the island."

"It's nice to meet you." Nancy held out her hand, noticing the congressman's red- and white-checked shirt and cowboy boots. His son wore deck shoes, jeans, and a blue polo shirt that matched the blue of his eyes. Not even the bruise on his cheek could spoil his incredible good looks, but his expression was tense, remote, and a little superior, Nancy thought.

"Pleased to meet you, ma'am," Winchester drawled. "A body, you said? Someone died?"

"Yes, sir. We believe it was one of our people— an Islander, that is. The next of kin is here now to make the identification." Jim nodded at a closed door behind the congressman.

"What happened? Another of those blasted moped accidents?" Winchester sounded irritated. "It's a wonder people aren't killed every day, the way the tourists drive."

"It wasn't an accident, sir. At least it doesn't appear that way, but I can't say more right now."

The congressman gave Jim a sharp glance. He reminded Nancy of an eagle—imposing, dignified, and ever watchful. "What's all this mystery?"

Jim cleared his throat. "It's just that we've barely begun our investigation and we're not able to discuss it yet. We'll be making an announcement as soon as the body has been officially identified by the victim's aunt."

"I see." Winchester nodded. "Thank you, Sergeant." He and his son walked away.

"Winchester is a very important person in New York politics," Jim told Nancy. "In fact, the rumor is he's about to be nominated as a judge on the state supreme court."

"It's interesting," Nancy said. "He sounds more like a Westerner than someone from New York."

"I understand that he moved up from Texas after his wife died some years ago. Apparently he lost a big election and blamed the other candidate for causing her heart attack. Claimed he waged a dirty campaign."

Nancy saw the door that Jim had indicated earlier was now opening. Others noticed it, too, and a hush fell over the room as the crowd waited for the next of kin to emerge.

A burly police officer appeared, supporting a small, plump, white-haired woman. The woman took a step forward, her face so white it resembled marble. Then her legs dissolved under her as she started to collapse in a faint.

"I know her!" Nancy whispered, her blue eyes widening. "That's Hannah's friend—the quilter, Sarah Windsor!"

Chapter

Three

THE OFFICER CAUGHT SARAH as she was falling. Jim ran over to help him put her into a chair, announcing in a loud voice, "That's it, folks. Please clear the room."

Nancy was about to help when the doctor she'd seen at the grave site appeared and bent over the older woman.

Jim returned to Nancy's side. "I'm sure she'll be fine once we get her home. But would you mind taking a rain check on that cup of coffee?"

"Sure. I should be getting back anyway. Maybe I'll see you tomorrow," she said, turning away.

Outside the station, Nancy collected Angie's moped, then slowly rode it into town. She left the moped in Angie's garage, along with a note of thanks, and walked on to the cottage.

Hannah was in the kitchen mixing a pitcher of

iced tea when Nancy arrived. "I walked down to the grocery store, but I only bought a few things. I thought we could eat out tonight—" Noticing Nancy's expression, she interrupted herself. "What's the matter?"

Nancy told her about the death of Sarah's nephew.

"I've got to go to her. Can you call a cab?" Hannah untied her apron. "Sarah lives off Corn Neck Road. Oh, poor dear, I know she was worried about him. She told me all about him, how he'd lost his parents and everything. She said he'd been gone since Friday night."

"Did she report him missing to the police?" Nancy asked, looking up taxicabs in the phone book.

"No. According to Sarah, he was a moody boy. He stayed with her, but he'd often go off for days at a time without a word."

Nancy wasn't surprised that Hannah knew so much about Tom, although she'd only met his aunt that morning. Total strangers often opened up to Hannah, sensing they could tell her anything. Nancy dialed the cab company and minutes later Hannah was off to comfort her new friend.

After that, Nancy called Barb. "I'm okay, Nancy, but I went over to talk to D. J. Divott and I'm awfully worried about him. He's awfully upset about Tom's death. They've been best friends since they were little kids."

"Is there anything I can do to help?"

"Thanks, but not now." Barb sighed. "I'd planned to take you to the Spotted Dog tonight. . . ."

"Don't worry about it," Nancy said.

"Wait, I have an idea for tomorrow," Barb said. "I always swim two miles when I finish work. Why don't you come to the beach with me tomorrow afternoon? We can lie in the sun and pretend this . . . murder never happened."

"Good idea." Nancy arranged to pick Barb up at her apartment the next day and hung up, then sank into a rocking chair on the porch.

Hannah returned at six and reported that Sarah's living room was full of friends who had come over to keep her company. She and Nancy decided to fix a simple supper of soup and sandwiches. A game of gin helped keep Nancy's mind off the murder during the evening, but as she fell asleep that night, she couldn't forget the image of Tom Haines's body buried in that lonely spot.

Right after breakfast Nancy and Hannah walked into town to the moped rental shop. Nancy rented a blue moped and was surprised when Hannah chose a bright red one. The shop owner suggested they practice in the large parking lot before going out on the road.

They donned their helmets and Nancy showed Hannah how to turn on the motor. She pointed to the right handlebar grip. "Think of that as your gas pedal. Turn it toward you, gently, like this, to give it a little gas."

Hannah twisted the grip and the motor roared. She jumped at the sound and let go of the handle. The engine automatically slowed.

"Not too much," Nancy said. Hannah tried again and the engine rose to a purr. "That's it. The levers on the handlebars are the brakes. When you want to slow down, release the gas and squeeze them."

"It seems easy," Hannah exclaimed. "It's just like riding a bike, without pumping."

Nancy smiled. "Right. Now start off slowly. Just give it the tiniest bit of gas."

Hannah took a deep breath. "Okay, here I go!" She puttered at two miles an hour around the lot, making a wide circle that arced back toward Nancy. "This isn't so hard!" she called. "It's *easier* than a bike!"

Nancy watched her make another wide turn. Suddenly the motor revved and Hannah shot back up the lot.

"Hit the brakes, Hannah!" Nancy shouted.

Hannah slowed only to make the turn around the row of parked cars. The bike tilted as she leaned into the curve. Then she raced back toward Nancy and skidded to a halt in front of her.

"I think I've got the hang of it," Hannah said, grinning.

"You scared me to death!" Nancy said, her heart still pounding.

"Don't worry about me, dear. I watch the road races on television all the time." Hannah patted Nancy's shoulder.

"Um, right, but control is important," Nancy reminded her. "Once we get out in traffic . . ."

"I'll be fine," Hannah said calmly. "Shall we hit the road?"

Nancy watched in amazement as Hannah negotiated her way through the busy downtown streets. It seemed as if she'd been riding all her life. Shaking her head in disbelief, Nancy wondered what other surprises Hannah had in store for her during the vacation.

At Hannah's insistence, they rode across the island to the Captain's Catch for lunch. Only a few tables were occupied in the dining room, but the deck overlooking Great Salt Pond was packed. Nancy and Hannah decided to wait for an outdoor table.

As she stood near the reservation stand, Nancy glanced around the restaurant, noticing the heavy tables, comfortable chairs, and dark wood paneling hung with pictures of old sailing ships. Nancy spotted the New York congressman, Walt Winchester, alone at a corner table. Just then a man in a business suit carrying a battered briefcase entered the restaurant and strode over to Winchester.

A few minutes later the hostess led Nancy and

Hannah to the deck. As they passed near Winchester, who was studying a typewritten sheet of paper, the man stood up, said goodbye, and began to walk away.

Nancy noticed he'd left his briefcase on the floor. "Sir," she called, but he didn't turn back. Nancy spoke to the congressman. "Your friend forgot his briefcase."

Winchester's face flashed annoyance, which vanished as soon as he recognized Nancy. "Why, Miss Drew, how nice to see you again." He stood and gave Nancy a courtly nod of his head, then glanced at the briefcase. "He didn't forget it. I'm afraid it's full of important—but tedious—documents for me to study. I can't escape from work, even when Congress is in recess."

Nancy smiled sympathetically. "May I introduce my friend, Hannah Gruen? Hannah, this is Congressman Walt Winchester."

"I'm pleased to meet you," he said, grinning. "In fact, it's a real privilege to meet such an attractive lady."

Hannah's cheeks grew pink. "It's nice to meet you, too, Congressman."

He glanced at his watch. "I'm afraid you'll have to excuse me. Have to fly back to Albany for a conference with the governor. My pilot is waiting at the airport."

"You have your own plane?" Hannah asked.

"Sure do," he replied affably as he pulled some bills out of his wallet and tossed them on the table. "Perhaps you might like to join me for a ride sometime, Ms. Gruen. We could hop over to Newport for lunch, or would you prefer Nantucket?"

"Well, either would be lovely, I'm sure," Hannah said graciously.

"Good, I look forward to it." With that, he picked up the briefcase and nodded to Nancy. "I must be off. Goodbye, ladies."

Nancy led a smiling Hannah to their table. When the waitress handed her a menu, Hannah read through it. "Heavens, look what they're charging for lobster salad!"

Nancy studied the face she had known since childhood, suddenly seeing Hannah in a new light. Her skin was unlined and the color of peaches and cream, her gray hair soft, her figure trim. No wonder a man like Walt Winchester would find her attractive.

Hannah leaned toward Nancy. "He's quite a charmer, isn't he?"

Nancy grinned. "Yes, he is. I understand he may be appointed a judge on the New York State Supreme Court."

"Really?" Hannah glanced at the menu. After a minute she said, "You know, I think I'll have that lobster salad."

After a leisurely lunch, the two of them separated. Hannah proudly rode her moped back to the cottage, and Nancy decided to stop by the police station before picking up Barb to go to the beach. She found Jim in his office, typing up a report.

"Hi," she said. "Got time to buy a girl a cup of coffee?"

The sergeant looked up from the computer screen. "Hi, Nancy. Gosh, I wish I could but we're swamped. How about a cup of the local brew instead?" He indicated the coffeemaker in the corner.

"Sure. I won't keep you. I just wondered how the case is going."

"Before we sent the hammer to the lab on the mainland for analysis, we noticed initials scratched into the handle. They led us to a suspect." He poured a cup of coffee and handed it to her. "He's being questioned right now."

Nancy was surprised. "That's fast work. Does that mean you think the hammer is the murder weapon?"

"The preliminary autopsy showed bruises on the face and head, but the cause of death was a sharp blow to the back of the skull. It will take a while to determine if the wound could have been caused by the hammer, but it seems likely."

"Bruises," Nancy said, thinking out loud. "Sounds like he must have been in a fight before he was killed."

"That's what we figure."

"Who is your suspect?" she asked.

Jim frowned. "Another Islander. They both fell for the same girl, and twice before this they tried to settle it with their fists. It's too bad—they used to be friends."

"Hathaway," a police officer called from the main room. "The chief wants you."

"On my way," Jim answered. "I've got to run, Nancy."

"See you later. And congratulations on solving the case so quickly."

Jim grinned and hurried away.

As Nancy rode her moped to Barb's apartment she felt a sense of relief that the case had apparently been solved so soon. Jim sounded confident that the lab would find evidence that the hammer was the murder weapon. She was ready to relax and enjoy her vacation, without the complication of a murder.

She was wearing a new bikini under her shorts and T-shirt, and had a towel and her tote bag stuffed in the moped's basket. She was anticipating a brisk swim followed by a lazy afternoon on the sand.

At the apartment Angie opened the door. "Hi," she said. "Barb should be here any minute. Come on in."

Nancy and Angie chatted while waiting for Barb. Nancy found out that the two had met at college in Boston, where Angie was majoring in art. Her father owned a pizza restaurant, a popular hangout for college students, and Angie worked there part-time, as did all her brothers and sisters. With her experience as a waitress, it had been easy to find a summer job on Block.

Without warning the door burst open and Barb charged in, furious. "You'll never believe what's just happened!"

"What?" Nancy asked, standing up.

"Do you know what the police have done now?"

"Why don't you tell us," Angie said calmly. She seemed to be used to Barb's outbursts.

"They picked up D. J. Divott. They think he murdered Tom!" Barb shouted.

"D.J.? Tom's best friend?" Angie said, clearly surprised.

"D.J. didn't do it, I know he didn't! They're arresting an innocent man! *And it's all my fault!*"

Chapter

Four

"WHY DO YOU THINK it's your fault?" Nancy asked.

Barb kicked a pillow across the room. "The police questioned me this morning. I had to tell them that I sort of dated Tom in June, and then I started going out with D.J. But they didn't listen when I said I wasn't serious about either one of them."

"Was Tom or D.J. serious about you?" Nancy asked.

"Of course not! We just hung out together."

"But, Barb," Angie said softly, "Tom and D.J. did get into a fight over you one night. I saw it."

"Oh, that was just plain silly," Barb said. "I don't think they were fighting over me, anyway. Those two had been squabbling since they were kids. They enjoyed it."

Nancy wondered if Barb was right. It was clear that she didn't take the rivalry seriously, but maybe Tom and D.J. had. She suspected that Barb didn't realize how attractive she was.

"Poor D.J.," Barb went on, pacing the room. "It's bad enough to lose Tom, and now the police accuse D.J. of his murder!"

"Barb," Nancy said. "The police have some strong evidence against D.J. Remember the hammer I found in the pond? Jim Hathaway told me it had D.J.'s initials on the handle."

"Lots of people must have the same initials," Barb argued. "The police are just grasping at straws. Half the business owners on the island were down at the station this morning, demanding action. They're afraid the tourists will be scared away if they think a murderer is on the loose."

"Well, they do have a point," Angie said quietly. "Tourists are Block's most important source of income."

Barb continued. "Just because they found a hammer with D.J.'s initials doesn't mean he's a killer. He's not! I know him!"

Nancy was impressed with Barb's conviction. She might be wrong, but if she was right, the police were after an innocent man.

"Nancy!" Barb swung around and placed both hands on Nancy's shoulders. "You're a detective. You can find out the truth. Please! Help him!"

"I don't know if I should get—"

"Sure you should! You can prove he's innocent. Just talk to him! You'll see!" Barb pleaded.

"Well, I guess I could talk to him. . . ." Nancy was almost smothered by Barb's hearty hug. Smiling at her enthusiasm, Nancy pulled away.

Barb frowned, worried again. "But when you see him, don't let him fool you, Nancy. He may be kind of gruff, but inside, he'll be really hurting. His best friend is dead and he can't deal with it yet."

"I understand," Nancy said. "Now, let's sit down and you can tell me more about Tom and D.J."

Half an hour later Nancy knocked on the door of D.J.'s office. Barb had given her directions to the barn on Old Town Road where he both lived and worked. The big red building had plenty of room for construction equipment on the ground floor next to the office, and an apartment upstairs.

Most of what Nancy had learned from Barb had to do with personal relationships but, before talking to him, she wanted some background on his business affairs.

As she expected, no one answered the door. Nancy tried the handle and found it unlocked. She let herself into the neat office. Apparently D.J. was organized and efficient, and the paperwork on various construction jobs showed that he was running a successful business as a contractor.

Barb had mentioned that Tom sometimes worked for D.J. and Nancy wanted to check it out. She found the payroll book in a drawer and opened it. Tom's name appeared fairly often over the past couple of years, but not once since the end of June. That was about the time Barb had stopped dating Tom and begun to go out with D.J.

Did D.J. fire Tom because of Barb? Or did Tom quit for the same reason? Nancy remembered Jim Hathaway saying that Tom had been flashing a lot of money around, so it looked as if he didn't need the job. And according to Barb, the two remained friendly, except for a few quarrels. But she'd also said both men were the type who tended to sulk, rather than discuss their feelings. Did those feelings finally explode in a fight that ended in murder? Or was there someone else angry enough at Tom to kill him?

It was time to talk to D.J., but first she had a few questions for Jim Hathaway.

Back at the police station, the dispatcher recognized Nancy and waved her through to Jim's office. He was on the phone, taking down a report of a missing dog. Nancy waited until he hung up.

"Hi. Hope I'm not interrupting," she said.

"You're a welcome interruption," he answered. "Can't wait till summer's over and the tourists give us back our island."

"I don't blame you." Nancy smiled. "Any new information on the case?"

"Several things. The coroner's report is in. Tom died on Friday night or early Saturday morning."

"Can you tell if he was murdered at the nature preserve?" Nancy asked.

"It was definitely at or near the grave site," Jim said. "I'll spare you the gruesome details that led to that conclusion."

"Thanks, I'll take your word for it." Nancy perched on the corner of Jim's desk. "How did he get to the nature preserve?"

"We found his motorcycle not far from the grave," Jim said.

"So he must have met someone there, they fought, and Tom was killed, either intentionally or accidentally," Nancy concluded.

"Yes, we know where and how it happened." Jim drummed his fingers on his desk. "But who did it? D.J.'s our main suspect, and we've warned him not to leave the island. But frankly, the things he told us led to more questions than answers."

"What do you mean?" Nancy asked.

"D.J. claims Tom borrowed the hammer months ago. He also said he wasn't with Tom the night he died but he saw him leaving the Spotted Dog with someone else."

"Who?"

"Believe it or not, Scott Winchester." Jim

noticed Nancy's look of surprise. "It doesn't make sense to us, either, except that we know D.J. isn't very fond of Scott. He may just be trying to make trouble for Scott."

Nancy couldn't help but wonder what the handsome rich boy and the Islander had in common. "How did the two of them know each other?"

"D.J. is building the Winchesters' house," Jim said. "He thinks Scott's a spoiled brat and can't stand taking orders from him."

"Do you know where D.J. is now?" Nancy was eager to question him.

"Gone fishing," Jim said with a wry grin. "I guess he's taking the rest of the afternoon off. I would, too, if I'd been picked up for murder."

"Do you know where?" Nancy asked.

"I heard the bluefish were running off Sandy Point. But, Nancy, I don't think you should talk to him alone. He's in a pretty surly mood right now."

"Don't worry, Jim, if the blues are running, I doubt we'll be alone."

Jim nodded. "That's true. Just be careful."

"Thanks. See you later."

Nancy hopped on her moped and rode across the island to Corn Neck Road, which ran north along the narrow strip of land connecting the upper and lower halves of Block. After she went past the dunes of Crescent Beach, the island grew broader. Houses and ponds dotted the countryside. Then a stone lighthouse came into view, standing where the road ended in a parking lot.

Nancy parked her moped and began to jog up the almost mile-long stretch of rocky beach. She passed a number of people fishing along the shore, casting their lines into the surf. Far ahead she could see the tiny spit of land called Sandy Point jutting out into the water. Where it ended, the currents of Block Island Sound on her left met those of the Atlantic Ocean to her right. Nancy had heard it was a favorite fishing spot, but it was also well known for its dangerous riptides.

Barb had described D.J. to Nancy. He was six-four, with a mop of thick, dark curly hair. She finally spotted him standing alone in the surf at the tip of Sandy Point. A black pickup truck was parked on the beach with no one else nearby. Panting slightly from her long jog, Nancy watched him send his line flying far out into the water, then slowly reel it in. The water came up to the knees of his waders, heavy rubber overalls.

She settled down on the beach to wait until he came back to shore, enjoying the warmth of the sun and the strong cool breeze blowing into her face. She watched the whitecaps form out in the Atlantic and gather strength as they rolled into shore. Some broke on a sandbar farther out.

Suddenly Nancy noticed the tip of D.J.'s rod bend in an arc. He reeled it in quickly, fighting the fish pulling against him. He played the fish expertly and in a short while waded back to shore, a foot-long bluefish in his net.

Nancy approached him as he dropped his catch in a bucket and bent down to remove the hook. "Hi, are you D. J. Divott?"

He raised up, scowling. "What if I am?"

"Barb Sommers asked me to talk to you. I'm Nancy Drew, and I thought if I could ask you a couple of questions—"

"You want to ask me questions?" D.J. savagely jerked the hook out of the fish's mouth. "Who do you think you are?"

Nancy put her hands on her hips. "I met Barb on the ferry yesterday and she thought I—"

"She's wrong!" D.J. said. "I've already answered more stupid questions than anyone should have to in a lifetime. Get lost, girl."

Nancy was annoyed. "If you'll stop being so rude and listen to what I have to say, I might be able to help you."

"You? Help me? Hah!" He stood up. "What are you going to do, waltz on down to the police station and bat your eyelashes at the cops?"

"Listen to me a minute! I'm a detective—"

"Don't make me laugh." He opened a coffee can and removed a chunk of cut-up fish.

"I am trying to *help* you!" Nancy said.

He jabbed the fishhook into the bait.

"I don't want your help. Buzz off." He walked back to the water, wading in until it came up above his knees.

Fuming, Nancy watched him go. He was one of the most obnoxious people she'd met in a long time. Then she remembered Barb's warning: "Don't let him fool you—inside he's really hurting."

Nancy sighed. Okay, she said to herself, I'll give him one more chance.

She sat down to wait until D.J. returned to shore, watching the waves roll in. One especially big whitecap formed out beyond the spot where D.J. stood. As she watched it dwarf the other waves, she realized D.J. was standing directly in its path.

Nancy jumped up and shouted a warning, but her voice was blown back on the wind. She began to run, knowing she couldn't reach him in time. The wave hit D.J., knocking him down in a wash of white foam. He struggled to his feet, then fell. Nancy realized that his waders were filling with water. He was helpless.

Again and again he tried to stand, but the surf kept pulling him under and the current was sweeping him out to sea. She scanned the beach, but everyone else was too far away to notice.

D.J. was drowning and she was the only one who could save him.

Chapter

Five

Nancy quickly stripped down to her bikini and plunged into the surf. She gasped when the cold spray hit her sun warmed skin. Battling against the current, she plunged through the water, bruising her feet on unseen rocks.

D.J. was being washed farther out to sea. He was now about twenty yards away.

As the water rose to her thighs Nancy felt the pull of the riptide grow stronger. Suddenly the bottom dropped away. She leapt forward and began to swim with fast, powerful strokes. Kicking hard, she closed the gap between them. Fifteen yards—ten . . .

D.J. was gasping for air, fighting to keep his head above water. Air pockets had formed inside his waders around his ankles, forcing his feet to the surface. At the same time, the weight of the water in his waders around his waist and chest was dragging the rest of his body under.

At last she reached D.J. As she wrapped him in a lifesaving hold, she felt her feet touch sand. Amazingly, the water only came up to her neck. They must be on a sandbar, she realized.

"You can touch bottom, D.J.!" she shouted. "Try to get your feet under you!"

He tried, but couldn't. One wave after another broke on them, knocking them around and burying them in white foam.

Knowing she had to do something before they were swept into deeper water, Nancy firmly dug her toes into the sand. Struggling desperately to keep D.J.'s head above water, she grabbed the straps of his waders and pushed them down off his shoulders. Then she began to peel the heavy material down his chest.

D.J. tried to help, but his feet kept bobbing to the surface. Nancy grabbed one boot and D.J. panicked. "I have to get the air out!" she yelled.

D.J. fell backward and his head went under for a moment. Nancy held tight to his thrashing foot. "Don't kick! Let me help you!"

She held on to it with both hands, squeezing tightly as she worked the air bubble up his leg. D.J. realized what she was doing and tried to keep his other leg still. When she finished with that leg, she started working the other one, pushing the air pockets out. Then she took a deep breath and dove, dragging his feet down to the sandbar. As she forced D.J. into an upright position, more bubbles worked their way free.

She surfaced and heard him shouting, "Over here! Hurry!"

Nancy turned to see a small fishing boat headed for them at top speed. It slowed when it reached them, giving Nancy the chance to take hold of the low gunwale to steady the boat against the breaking waves. Two men reached down and grabbed D.J.'s arms.

"Go around to the other side to help balance us!" one of the men told Nancy. She swam to the far side of the boat and held on to the edge. A third man leaned over on the same side, adding his weight to hers.

The two men reaching for D.J. paused a second, waiting for the next wave to help lift him. Timing it, they shouted, "One, two, three, heave!"

Nancy pulled down on the boat with all her strength. The hull rose up, lifting her almost clear of the water. D.J. was dragged over the side. The men grabbed his legs and flipped him into the bottom of the boat.

The little vessel righted itself. "Now you, young lady." The third man grasped her under the arms and easily lifted her aboard.

Nancy sank down onto a cushioned seat, her breath coming in fast gasps. One of the men handed her a towel. "That was good work, miss. He owes his life to you."

"And to you, too," Nancy said, wiping salt-water off her face. "We sure were glad to see you coming."

"He wouldn't have lasted till we got here if you hadn't helped. I saw a man drown in the same kind of accident. Once those waders are full of water it's like wearing a concrete suit."

"Hey, fella"—one of the other men poked D.J.—"aren't you going to say thank you to this lady?"

D.J. sat in the bottom of the boat, next to a bucket of bait. His head was in his hands, the waders still binding his legs. Now he glanced up at Nancy and muttered, "Thanks."

"Guess he needs a little time to recover," one of the men said as he put the boat in gear and started back to the beach.

D.J. was embarrassed. "Sorry." He began to work his feet free of the waders. "Th-thanks, all of you."

"No problem, buddy." The man beside him slapped him on the back.

"How did you know we needed help?" Nancy asked.

"Someone spotted you from the lighthouse and radioed us," the man said. "We were fishing around the point. Glad we made it in time."

Nancy smiled gratefully. "So are we."

When they reached shore, Nancy and D.J. slowly walked back to the spot where D.J. had left his things. Nancy could see D.J. was exhausted, so she silently picked up some of his fishing gear and carried it to his pickup truck. She noticed a sticker on the windshield, authorizing him to drive on the beach.

"You want a ride back?" D.J. asked when everything was loaded.

"Sure, let me pick up my clothes. I left my moped in the lot." Nancy pulled her T-shirt over her wet bathing suit and climbed into the front seat. She glanced at his haggard face as they drove down the beach. She hoped he'd be willing to talk to her soon, but now wasn't the time to question him about his best friend's murder.

"Uh, well . . ." he said as he pulled up next to her moped. "I mean . . . thanks."

Nancy got out and watched him drive away. She shook her head, a thin smile on her lips. Some people sure have a way with words, she thought.

Hannah wanted to cancel their dinner reservation when Nancy told her about the rescue. "I'm glad you saved that poor man, but you must be worn-out. I think you need a quiet night at home."

"I'm fine, Hannah, and I've been looking forward to dinner at the Bell Buoy. They say it's the best place in town for shrimp scampi."

Hannah shook her head, but she couldn't hide

a small smile. As the sun began to dip over the west side of the island, they rode down the hill to the restaurant near the docks in Old Harbor.

When the hostess showed them to their table in the busy restaurant, Nancy was pleased to find that Angie was their waitress. She looked especially pretty, dressed all in white with a blue Bell Buoy apron and a matching blue ribbon in her long dark hair.

"Hi, Angie. I didn't know you were working tonight." Nancy took the menu Angie handed her.

"I wasn't supposed to, but one of the girls is sick," Angie said. "They called me because they know I'm always happy to make the extra money."

"Hannah," Nancy said. "This is Barb Sommers's roommate, Angelina Cassetti."

"Hello," Hannah said. "Nancy has told me about you."

Angie smiled, then turned back to Nancy. "I heard about you rescuing D.J. today. He told Barb you saved his life."

"How is Barb?" Nancy asked, anxious to change the subject. She hated to worry Hannah, and hadn't yet told her that she was investigating the murder.

"Barb is . . . well, not so good," Angie said. "On top of everything else, they've discovered that one of the burying beetle nests was destroyed when that grave was dug. It's a real disaster, because there are so few of them to begin with."

"That's a shame," Nancy said.

Angie saw someone signaling her at another table. "I've got to go. Do you like swordfish? It's very fresh tonight—just off the boat." She hurried away.

"Swordfish sounds good," Hannah said.

After they finished consulting their menus, Nancy asked Hannah about Sarah.

"She's managing, but it's difficult," Hannah said. "I stopped by Crazy for Crafts this afternoon. Thank goodness, the shop keeps her busy, but she's still upset. With the body being held for the autopsy, she doesn't know when she can have a funeral."

Just then Angie returned to take their orders.

"Hannah will have the swordfish," Nancy said. "And I'll try the scampi."

Angie wrote it down, collected their menus, and said, "Gosh, Nancy, I'm so glad you're looking into this murder. Poor Barb has been hit with one thing after another—the murder, the beetles, now D.J. almost drowning. It helps her to know that you're going to find out who killed Tom." She sighed and left.

Hannah frowned at Nancy. "You didn't mention you were checking into this murder."

Nancy blushed slightly and said, "I was going to tell you. I just didn't want you to worry."

"And why *shouldn't* I worry?" Hannah said. "You go risking your life, tracking down criminals—"

"There really isn't any danger, Hannah," Nancy assured her. "I'm only asking a few questions because Barb really wants me to help out. She's sure D.J. is innocent. It's important to everyone, especially Sarah, that we find out the truth."

Hannah sighed. "Poor Sarah. Not knowing is so hard on her. All right, Nancy, I see your point. Only promise me you'll be careful."

"I promise," Nancy said.

Nancy changed the subject while they ate, concentrating on their plans for when George and Bess arrived. They finished up by ordering two slices of double-fudge cake.

Angie was serving them their desserts when she stopped and gasped out loud. Nancy turned to see what she was staring at. Walt and Scott Winchester were following the hostess to one of Angie's tables.

After the Winchesters were seated, Angie turned away from Nancy and Hannah, stopping the hostess as she passed by. "I can't serve that party," Angie said, sounding desperate. "Please put them somewhere else."

"That's the only free table, and they've been waiting for twenty minutes," the hostess said.

Angie's face was white with tension. "You don't understand. *I absolutely can't serve them!*"

The hostess's eyes hardened. "Sorry, but you've got to."

Angie stood still, her lips quivering. Without warning she untied her apron, dropped it to the floor, and ran out of the restaurant.

Chapter

Six

ASTONISHED, NANCY WATCHED Angie rush out of the restaurant.

"Do you know what's wrong, Nan?" Hannah asked.

"I have no idea." Nancy studied the Winchesters, wondering which of them Angie couldn't stand, father or son. The two men were so involved in a discussion—or was it an argument?—that they apparently hadn't noticed anyone else in the restaurant.

Nancy couldn't imagine what Angie could have against Walt Winchester, but Scott was easy. He was so handsome, so arrogant. His smile was forced, even with his father.

What was the connection between Angie and Scott? Maybe he'd asked her out, or dated her for a while, then dumped her. Whatever it was, he must have treated her badly.

Nancy resolved to ask Barb about it the next day.

Barb called in the morning and suggested a picnic lunch at Mohegan Bluffs. Nancy rode over to the Nature Conservancy near Great Salt Pond to pick her up a little before noon.

"Hi," Barb said when Nancy stepped into the office to the right of the door. "Let me grab some food out of the refrigerator and we'll be off. I can't wait to show you the cliffs."

She disappeared into a back room and returned a moment later with a paper bag that she was stuffing in her knapsack.

"How's your work going?" Nancy asked, avoiding the delicate subject of D.J. and Tom.

"Everyone is still upset about the nest that was destroyed," Barb said as they went out to their mopeds. "All the babies were killed, although it's possible the parents escaped."

"If they did, will they mate again?" Nancy asked.

"Maybe, but it's late in the breeding season." Barb mounted her bike. "Enough shop talk. I need to get away and not think about D.J. or Tom or anything. I'd like to try to have a little fun!"

Nancy followed Barb to Center Street and up into the hills toward the southern end of the island. They passed a number of freshwater ponds as well as the airport.

Finally Barb slowed and turned off onto a narrow lane. When it ended, they left their mopeds and followed a path through wild rosebushes to the edge of a high cliff.

"Wow, what a sight," Nancy said. Off to her left was the redbrick Southeast Lighthouse and before her was a steep cliff that dropped down a couple hundred feet to a rocky shore below. A strong wind was kicking up whitecaps far out and choppy waves rolled into shore.

"I love watching the ocean from here," Barb said. "Do you realize, if you started swimming from here the first land you'd reach would be Portugal?"

"I'm a good swimmer, *but* . . ." Nancy smiled.

"Why don't we eat our lunch here, then walk down the path to the beach."

Nancy checked out the narrow trail that snaked its way down the cliff. "How do you walk down a cliff that's almost vertical?"

"Never fear, the most dangerous part of the trail is the poison ivy growing along the sides."

Grinning, Nancy said, "Now you've got me worried."

Barb sat down on the grass and dug their lunch out of her knapsack. "There's a staircase closer to the lighthouse, but I like this spot. Angie and I discovered it, and not too many people know about it." She shivered slightly and zipped up her windbreaker. "Wow, the wind is strong."

"The radio said a storm is on the way. It's

supposed to hit sometime this evening," Nancy said, taking the tuna sandwich Barb handed her.

Barb opened a bag of potato chips, then stared thoughtfully at the high white clouds scudding across the sky. Finally Barb broke the silence and spoke about what was on both of their minds. "I saw D.J. last night. I want to thank you again for rescuing him, Nancy. He's not too swift with words, as you might have noticed, but he *was* grateful."

"Maybe now he'll talk to me," Nancy said.

"I asked him to cooperate, but he's funny, full of stiff-necked Yankee pride. Plus, he was really shaken by Tom's death, and furious that anyone could think he might have killed him."

Nancy took a bite of her sandwich. "But they did fight a lot. Maybe this fight got out of hand and Tom was killed accidentally."

"Don't let D.J. hear you say that," Barb warned. "Look, he's building a house not far from here. We'll stop by on our way back, but be careful. Right now he's a keg of dynamite—with a short fuse."

They were quiet for a while, eating and watching the boats bobbing in the rough water far down below.

"Something odd happened last night," Nancy said after a few minutes. She told Barb about Angie's strange behavior in the restaurant. "Did Scott and Angie ever date?"

"They sure did," Barb said. "For a long time.

They met last fall in college, and when Scott dropped out of school this spring and came to Block, Angie followed him as soon as the semester was over. They really seemed to be in love, so I was surprised when they broke up last month."

"He must have done something pretty awful for Angie to get so upset."

Barb shrugged. "I guess so. She refuses to talk about it or him."

"Why did Scott drop out of college?" Nancy asked, curious about the handsome blond with the superior air.

"I don't know him very well, but Angie once told me that he was getting a lot of pressure from his father to study pre-law. He didn't like it."

"Dropping out isn't any way to solve a problem," Nancy said.

"Maybe there was more to it. I only knew him through Angie, and she and I weren't really close until we began sharing the apartment this summer."

By the time they finished eating, they were both chilled by the wind. "Let's climb down to the beach another time, Barb," Nancy said. "I'd like to talk to D.J. right now."

"Fine with me," Barb said, packing up their litter. "Besides, this wind must be blowing close to thirty knots. It'll be more fun on a calm day."

They mounted their mopeds and headed north. Soon after they passed a large lake called

Fresh Pond, Barb turned into an unpaved driveway and Nancy followed her up a steep hill to a huge house under construction. Perched on one of the highest spots on the island, it overlooked rolling fields, ponds, and the sea beyond.

They parked next to a small trailer that Barb explained served as D.J.'s temporary office.

As Nancy turned off her moped, she spotted Scott Winchester coming out the front door. "I think it's great that D.J. is building the congressman's house," she said to Barb.

"Yes, it's the best commission he's had in a long time. It's an incredible house—everything is custom designed and built by hand, even ordinary things like the window frames." She turned and shouted, "Hey, D.J.!"

D.J. was standing, staring up at the roof. When he saw Barb, he waved. "Be with you in a minute! No, Hank, not that way," he yelled to a short, dark-haired man. "Try it from the other side."

The carpenters were all busy, struggling in the strong wind to fasten huge blue tarps over the only partially roofed house before the storm hit. Scott strode around the site, making suggestions and lending a hand here and there. D.J. kept throwing him angry glances. It was obvious he resented Scott's interference, but Scott didn't seem to notice.

As Nancy and Barb joined D.J., Scott checked his watch and joined them. "Divott, I figure we'll still have an hour or so once the tarps are in place. How about installing the sliding glass doors before we call it quits for the day?"

"It's too late and windy to start that project now," D.J. said crisply.

"But my father wanted—" Scott began.

"I don't care. I'm in charge here and I say it can't be done," D.J. snapped.

Scott shrugged and took off, frowning.

Just then a red sports car zoomed up the driveway. Walt Winchester was at the wheel. As he got out, Scott went over to him.

D.J. watched them and said to Barb, "I ought to walk out on this job. I would, too, except Winchester would sue my socks off if I tried."

Barb shrugged, then smiled. "Do you have a minute? Nancy has a couple of questions to ask you."

D.J. seemed ready to refuse, then he sighed and said, "Okay, but only a minute." He glanced around to make sure nobody could overhear them.

"Tom worked with you, on and off, until the end of June, is that right?" Nancy asked.

"Yeah, when he wasn't working on a boat. He liked them better than houses."

"Is that why he stopped working for you? He found a job on a boat?"

"Not exactly," D.J. said suspiciously. "Why are you asking?"

"I was just curious," Nancy said casually. "I understand he was spending quite a bit of money this summer and I wondered what he was doing to earn it."

"It's none of your business," D.J. said coldly.

Nancy said, "I'm only asking because—"

"I don't care why you're asking!" D.J. hissed. "Leave Tom alone! He's dead!"

"But—"

"Look, I never ratted on Tom while he was alive and I'm sure not going to start now!" he shouted. "I don't care if you *are* a detective! You keep your nose out of this!" He stalked off.

Nancy turned to get Barb's reaction and realized the Winchesters were standing nearby. Had they overheard D.J.'s last words?

"Miss Drew, we meet again," Walt Winchester said courteously.

"Hello, Congressman. Do you know Barb Sommers?" Nancy said.

"Pleased to meet you, Miss Sommers." He shook her hand.

"You're building a beautiful house, Mr. Winchester," Barb said. "And what a terrific view you'll have."

"Thank you. We're pleased with it," he said.

"Dad," Scott said, "I've got to leave. I, uh, I'm supposed to meet someone about the, uh, plumbing fixtures."

"Okay," his father said. "When you get back to

the boat later, check the extra anchor to make sure it's holding. If the wind shifts, you'll have to adjust the angle."

"All right." Scott went over to speak to a worker, then took off on his moped.

"Well, I'd better make sure the house is battened down as well as the boat. Please excuse me." Winchester left to inspect his property.

"Well, now what?" Barb said to Nancy.

"Do you think if we stay a little longer D.J. will calm down and talk to me?" Nancy asked.

Barb shrugged. "I don't know. We can only try."

Half an hour later D.J. dismissed the work crew, but when Barb approached him, he stalked off, obviously still angry.

Nancy started up her moped. "I've been thinking. I'm sure the key to this case has to be the money Tom was flashing around this summer."

"You think it's connected with his death?" Barb asked as she adjusted her helmet strap.

"If we find the source of the money, we'll know what he was up to. That may tell us why someone wanted to kill him. You've got to work on D.J., Barb. Get him to talk to me."

"I'll try." She revved her engine. "Ready?"

Nancy nodded and they started back to town. Clouds rolled across the sun, dark and ominous, but her mind was so preoccupied with the case, Nancy hardly noticed. She was convinced that D.J. knew how Tom had been getting his money.

If she could only get him to talk to her, that information might lead her to the killer.

They were rounding a curve when Nancy heard the roar of a motorcycle behind them. She moved over to give it room to pass.

Seconds later she felt a tremendous jolt and thud against the back of her moped. The bike leapt sideways and Nancy was thrown off it and into the air!

Chapter

Seven

REMEMBERING HER JUDO TRAINING, Nancy tucked her head, wrapped her arms around her chest, and relaxed her muscles. She hit hard on her right shoulder at the grassy edge of the road. The force of the impact sent her rolling down an embankment.

At last she came to a halt, stopped by a thick hedge of wild blackberry bushes. The thorns scratched through her thin windbreaker and clung to her as she tried to pull away. She stopped fighting and lay still for a moment, catching her breath.

"Nancy!" Barb ran down the embankment. "Are you all right?"

"Yes," she said calmly. "Except I'm being attacked by a bush."

"How can you joke at a time like this?" Barb

knelt down and began to pull the thorns from Nancy's clothes.

As soon as she was free, Nancy slid away from the hedge and sat up slowly. "No broken bones, just a few bruises. I'm glad I was wearing a helmet. Did you get a look at that motorcycle?"

"Only a glimpse, but I'm sure I'd recognize it if I saw it again," Barb said. "It was black, with a yellow streak of lightning painted on the side. I couldn't see the driver's face, because he was wearing a dark helmet visor."

Nancy stood up. "Is my moped wrecked?"

"I didn't stop to check. Are you sure you can walk?" Barb asked anxiously.

"Yes, I'm fine," Nancy said. "Come on, let's go. I want to find the idiot who hit me."

When they found Nancy's moped, it was lying on its side, still running, the rear wheel spinning uselessly. They checked it over. It was dented and scraped but still rideable.

"Let's head for town," Nancy said. "That's the most likely place he'd go, to try to lose himself in a crowd."

"I can't believe anyone wouldn't stop to see if you were all right."

"They call it hit-and-run," Nancy said grimly. The question is, she added to herself, was the attack deliberate? Unless he was incredibly incompetent, why had he hit her when he had room to pass, a dry road, and no traffic in sight? I want to find that guy, she said to herself.

They rode back to Old Harbor, scanning the traffic as they went.

Finally Barb said, "I'm beginning to think it's useless. He could be anywhere on the island by now."

"Or even *off* the island, if he caught a ferry." Nancy checked her watch. "It's three twenty-five. What time does the ferry leave?"

"There's one at three-thirty," Barb said.

"Hurry, let's get down to the dock."

By the time they worked their way through the traffic, the ferry's whistle was blowing, signaling its departure. Nancy and Barb jumped off their mopeds and ran toward it, but were stopped by the barrier at the end of the pier.

"Did you see someone with a black motorcycle board the boat?" Nancy asked the girl who collected tickets at the barrier. "It had a streak of yellow lightning painted on the side."

"Yeah, sharp machine," the girl said, chewing gum.

"Please, I've got to talk to the driver. Can you let me through?" Nancy said.

"Got a ticket?" the girl asked.

"No, but—"

"No ticket, you don't get through." The girl snapped her gum. "Those are the rules."

Nancy glanced at the ticket office, but the crew was already pulling up the boarding ramp, and by the time she got back it would be too late. She pressed forward, straining at the barrier, trying to spot the motorcycle.

"I think I see it," Barb said, excited. "Look on the right, beside the blue car."

"You're right!" Nancy said. "And look who's standing next to the motorcycle! Isn't that one of the construction workers on D.J.'s crew?"

"Yes," Barb said. "Didn't D.J. call him Hank?"

Nancy cupped her hands around her mouth. "Hey, Hank!" she shouted. "Hank!"

The man, who was short with a dark suntan, saw her. Surprised, he pushed his way to the stern of the ferry. "What do you want?"

"You sideswiped my moped!" Nancy yelled.

Hank laughed. Most of his answer was drowned out by the ferry's whistle as it pulled away from the dock. All Nancy heard was "Crazy dumb tourist. Why don't you learn how to ride?" He turned and disappeared into the crowd of passengers.

Frustrated, Nancy watched the ferry move out to open water. She pounded her fist on the barrier. "He's not going to get away with this! I'm going to report him to the police. They can have someone pick him up when he arrives at Point Judith."

They rode over to the police station. Jim smiled when he saw Nancy, but he became serious as he listened to her story.

"The road was perfectly clear," Nancy finished. "There was no reason for him to hit me."

"This doesn't sound good." Jim frowned. "Fill out a report and I'll call the mainland right away."

Nancy wrote out a detailed report. Jim told her to check back around five, after the ferry had docked.

"Nancy, I've got to stop by the Nature Conservancy office," Barb said as they went out of the police station.

"Okay, I think I'd better take my moped to the rental shop. It's making a funny noise, and I should tell them about the accident." She waved goodbye to Barb.

By the time Nancy dealt with the insurance claims and exchanged her moped for another, it was close to five o'clock. She returned to the police station.

Jim shook his head when he saw her come in. "It's the strangest thing," he said. "The guy you're looking for seems to have vanished. A state trooper boarded the ferry as soon as it docked, ready to pick up whoever claimed the motorcycle. No one showed up. The guy must have walked off the boat with the other passengers, leaving his cycle behind."

"You're kidding," Nancy said, amazed. "It's practically a brand-new bike." Nancy paused, staring at the large map of the island on the wall. "That confirms it. I'm sure he meant to hit me."

"There's no doubt something fishy's going on," Jim said. "I'll check with D. J. Divott, since he hired the guy. I'll get a last name, address, and so on. Don't worry, we'll pick him up soon."

"Thanks, Jim." Nancy walked out to her moped and stood there in the cold wind, thinking. Hank had just walked off the ferry. No one would abandon an almost new motorcycle unless someone had paid him enough to make it worth his while. But *who* might have paid Hank to run her off the road? D.J.? If he killed Tom, he had a good reason to stop her from investigating the case. Just because Barb was sure he was innocent didn't mean he was.

Then, too, anyone at the construction site could have heard D.J. shouting that she was a detective. What had happened next? Nancy thought back. Scott had left soon afterward. In fact, it sounded as if he'd made up an excuse to leave. And *before* he left, he had spoken to some of the workers. Was Hank one of them? Nancy couldn't remember.

She shook her head. According to D.J., Scott was the last person to see Tom alive. But why would Scott kill Tom?

As far as Nancy was concerned, it all came back to the money. Where and how had Tom gotten it? Who had plenty of money to give to him, for whatever he was doing? Scott Winchester, for one.

Nancy shivered as the wind whipped reddish

blond curls off her neck. The sky was low and gray overhead and it appeared as if the storm were moving in fast. She wondered if Scott had returned to the yacht where he and his father lived. Great Salt Pond, where they were anchored, was just down the road from the police station. She decided to take a look.

She rode the short distance and strolled out to the end of their dock.

All over the harbor people were preparing for the storm. Those whose boats were tied to the piers were busy doubling up on their docking lines. Canvas awnings were removed, lines wrapped around the sail covers, fuel and water tanks filled. Dinghies bustled back and forth on the pond as supplies were ferried out to the moorings.

Nancy checked to her left, where a longer dock stretched out into the huge harbor. She spotted Walt Winchester striding past a line of cabin cruisers and sailboats. He reached a ladder and climbed down, untying a dinghy.

Nancy's eyes were then drawn to a white yacht moored about two hundred yards in front of her. The yacht was at least fifty feet long, with lovely clean lines. The name, painted on the stern in gold letters, was *Emily Sue*.

As she watched, someone in a yellow hooded slicker ran out on the yacht's deck, climbed into an old wooden rowboat tied to the stern, and quickly pulled away. Nancy lost track of it as it zigzagged among the many anchored boats.

Walt Winchester had started up the small outboard motor on his dinghy. He set a course straight for the white yacht.

The rowboat reappeared from behind a small sloop and headed for a narrow beach on Nancy's left. Just as it pulled ashore, a gust of wind blew back the hood of the slicker and Nancy saw that it was Angie.

Two kids were sitting on the dock several feet away from her. One of them turned around, and she saw it was Ashley Hanna, the pretty, dark-haired girl from the ferry.

"Hi, Nancy," she called out. "What are you doing here?"

"Just admiring the boats," Nancy answered. "Do you know who owns the yacht *Emily Sue?*" She pointed it out.

"No, but maybe my cousin does," said Ashley.

"Sure, that's Congressman Winchester's boat," the older boy said. "He and his son live on it."

"Thanks," Nancy said, frowning. So Walt was definitely headed for his yacht, and it seemed as if Angie had left the very same boat in a hurry.

Angie, who refused to wait on the Winchesters in the restaurant. Angie, who had once dated Scott Winchester and now apparently hated him.

What in the world had she been doing on the *Emily Sue?*

Chapter

Eight

NANCY WATCHED as Angie landed the rowboat. She quickly shoved the oars under the seat, then whipped the mooring line around a metal ring sunk into the sand. Before Nancy could start after her, she ran across the beach to a parking area, jumped on her moped, and roared off.

What possible reason did Angie have to be on board the Winchesters' yacht? Nancy asked herself. Was Scott there? Had she gone to talk to him?

Just then Walt Winchester's dinghy reached the yacht and he climbed on board. About ten minutes later Nancy saw him emerge on deck, carrying a small overnight bag. When he arrived back at the pier, he handed the dock boy some money and pointed at his dinghy, named *SueSue*.

Now Nancy was sure Scott was on board. The

congressman was obviously asking the dock boy to return the dinghy to the yacht. If Scott were ashore, he'd leave the *SueSue* at the pier so his son could get out to the yacht.

Nancy said a hurried farewell to Ashley and hurried over to the adjoining dock. With all the bustle on the pier, Winchester didn't notice her pass him as he headed for the parking lot.

The dock boy tied another dinghy to *SueSue*'s stern and started up the motor. Nancy reached him just before he pulled away.

"Hi," Nancy said. "Can I hitch a ride?"

"Sure, where are you headed?" he asked.

Nancy improvised quickly. "I'm supposed to meet Scott Winchester on his yacht."

"Hop aboard then. That's where I'm going."

It was a bumpy, wet ride, with the wind blowing the spray from whitecaps into Nancy's face. When they reached the yacht, Nancy scrambled up the ladder. "Hello," she called. "May I come aboard?"

Scott Winchester emerged from the cabin, wearing jeans and an old sweatshirt. The bruise on his cheek was beginning to fade.

"What are you doing here?" Scott was clearly surprised to see her.

Nancy grinned. "Oh, I was in the neighborhood and thought I'd stop by."

Scott smiled slightly. "Come on into the cabin."

Nancy followed him down the companionway

steps and looked around the main room. It was paneled in mahogany, with comfortable swivel chairs around a dining table. On the right was a navigator's desk and beyond it an efficient galley.

"What a beautiful boat," Nancy said.

"I'm glad you like her. She was named after my mother," Scott said softly.

Nancy heard the note of sadness in his voice, but noticed that he seemed more relaxed than she expected, even friendly.

"Uh, would you like a soda or something?" Scott asked. "Have a seat."

"Thanks, I'd love one," Nancy said, sitting in one of the swivel chairs.

Scott pulled a can out of the refrigerator, popped the top, and handed it to her. "What can I do for you?"

"I've been wanting to talk to you," Nancy said. "I saw your father leave as I was headed out here, so I thought this might be a good time. Do you expect him back soon?"

"No, he's flying to Albany before the storm hits. He has a number of meetings scheduled for tomorrow." Scott sounded wary. "What did you want to talk to me about?"

"Barb Sommers is worried because the police think D. J. Divott killed Tom Haines," Nancy began gently. "I promised her I'd ask around to see if anyone knows anything more about the murder."

"You're a detective, aren't you?" Scott said. "I heard D.J. call you that at the construction site this afternoon."

"I've had some detective experience, but this is nothing official," Nancy said casually, taking a sip of soda. "I'm just trying to help Barb out."

Scott sat down at the table, fingering a worn, folded sheet of paper he'd pulled from his pocket. "Why do you think I know anything about the murder?"

"Someone saw you leaving the Spotted Dog with Tom about nine o'clock on the night he was killed." Nancy held her breath. Would Scott blow up?

"Oh, that." To her relief, Scott didn't seem upset. "I've already explained it to the police. We didn't leave together. We just happened to go out the door at the same time. He asked me how the house was coming along, and I told him about a small problem we were having with the plumbing."

"But I heard that you two rode off together," Nancy said, wondering if Scott got the bruise on his cheek in a fight with Tom.

"I followed him as far as the junction," Scott said. "He turned toward town and I headed back here to the yacht."

It was a believable story, Nancy thought. Still, she detected a certain tension in Scott, especially when he talked about returning to the yacht. She decided not to press the point right then, especially since he had dropped his remote, superior air and was willing to talk to her.

"Did you know Tom well?" Nancy asked.

"Not really." Scott toyed with the worn piece of paper. It had been folded and unfolded so many times the creases had worn through in spots. "He was just one of the construction workers. Once in a while I'd see him at the Spotted Dog."

"Still, the murder must have been quite a shock," Nancy said.

"Yeah. Sure. It was."

Nancy heard the remoteness creeping back into his voice and decided it was time to change the subject. She took a sip of soda and leaned back in her chair. "How did you like your dinner at the Bell Buoy the other night? I thought the scampi was delicious."

"Were you there?" Scott said, surprised. "I didn't notice you."

"We were having dessert when you arrived," Nancy said. "The food was great, and so was the service. Angelina Cassetti was our waitress."

"*Angie?*" Scott sat up straight. "I didn't see her. She wasn't supposed—"

Nancy waited for him to finish, but he'd clamped his mouth shut. "Barb said you and Angie dated for a while."

"Uh, yeah, we did." A slow flush crept up his cheeks. "But we don't now."

"That's too bad," Nancy said. "I like her very much. She's lovely."

"Yes, she's—very lovely," Scott said softly.

Nancy was amazed. She'd expected anger, indifference—almost anything but Scott's wistful praise. "Barb said you know Angie from college."

"Yes." He frowned at the folded paper.

"Did you meet in class?" Nancy asked.

"No, in her father's pizza shop. She works there as a waitress part-time." He paused, then suddenly rushed on. "All her brothers and sisters help out in the restaurant. But Angie's so smart, she shouldn't have to work. She should be able to spend all her time on her courses—"

He abruptly stopped and glanced shyly at Nancy. "I don't know why I'm telling you all this."

"It's fascinating," Nancy said.

"Are you *really* a detective?"

"I've solved a few cases," she said, then smiled. "But I've never been able to solve the mystery of love."

"Who has?" Scott said thoughtfully.

"You were telling me about Angie and how hard she works."

"I'm not blaming her parents, you know," he said in quick protest. "They're great people and they treat me like one of their family. And her dad let Angie come to Block Island this summer, even though he really needed her help."

Nancy listened, thinking how different Scott was from her first impression of him. Talking about Angie, he was open and warm. He almost sounded as if he were still in love with her. She wondered if she dared to ask him about Angie's visit to the yacht, but she decided not to risk it.

"One reason Tony's Pizza is so popular," he continued, "is because her dad's a super guy. . . ."

Nancy sipped her soda while Scott told her about Angie's brothers and sisters and her mother's incredible lasagna. Finally she glanced at her watch and said, "Wow, I didn't realize it was so late. I'd better be going."

Scott stuffed the folded paper in the pocket of his jeans. "I'll give you a ride to shore." He cocked his head, listening for a moment. "I'd better lend you a foul weather jacket. Sounds like the wind has picked up."

Nancy fastened the yellow slicker over her windbreaker and followed him up on deck. Scott was right—the wind was even stronger than earlier. Over its roar, Nancy heard the chimes of a hundred wire halyards slapping against metal masts all over the harbor.

"The radio said this was going to be quite a storm," Nancy said as they climbed into the *SueSue*. "Are you planning to ride it out on board?"

"I told my father I would." Scott pulled at the loose neckline of his jacket as if it were choking him. Was he worried about the storm? "Someone has to be here in case of trouble."

"Wouldn't you rather take a room on shore for the night?" Nancy asked.

Scott grinned. "I'd only lie awake worrying about *Emily Sue.*" He started the motor and headed for the pier. When they reached the dock, Nancy grabbed the ladder to steady the boat. "Thanks for the soda. Maybe I'll see you around."

"Hey, listen," Scott said. "You won't say anything about . . . uh . . ."

"Angie? Of course not." She took off the slicker he'd given her and handed it to him. "I'm a good listener, but I'm not a gossip."

"Yeah, I might have guessed that. I don't usually . . ." He shrugged, embarrassed.

Nancy smiled. "Thanks again—I really enjoyed seeing your boat." She stepped onto the ladder at the dock.

"Come back sometime and I'll give you the grand tour," Scott promised.

"I'd like that." She waved goodbye, headed for her moped, and rode toward home. She planned to talk to Scott again soon, now that he had opened up to her. She still needed to ask him how he got that bruise on his cheek, and why did he tense up when she asked him about the murder?

Nancy was sure he was hiding something.

What was more, the mystery of Scott and Angie's relationship had only deepened. Why had Angie been on his boat? And why did she appear to hate Scott when he spoke of her with such affection? She decided to call Barb to see if she could remember more about their breakup.

She had just parked the moped in the garage behind the cottage when Hannah burst out the door.

"Nancy! I'm so glad you're back!" Hannah said.

"What's the matter?"

"It's Sarah! I just called her and she was crying too hard to talk. Something's happened." Hannah buttoned up her raincoat. "I'm going over to her house right away!"

"I'll come with you!"

Hannah led the way to Sarah's old farmhouse on Corn Neck Road. Sarah answered their knock after a minute, tears running down her cheeks. She hugged Hannah. "I'm so glad you came! I didn't know what to do!"

"What happened?" Nancy asked.

"I—I was looking for a suit—you know, to bury Tom in—if we can ever schedule the funeral. And in the back of his closet, I found this!"

Sarah picked up a cardboard shoe box. Inside it was money. Lots of money. Thousands of dollars. In cash.

Chapter

Nine

"WHERE DID TOM get all this money?" Sarah wailed, showing the box to Nancy and Hannah. The bills were all used, tens and twenties and fifties, all jumbled together. "He had to be doing something really bad."

"Why don't you come sit down, Sarah," Hannah said, leading her into the living room. Nancy followed, noticing the pretty quilted pillows, hand-knit afghans, and embroidered doilies that brightened up the somewhat worn furniture.

Sarah tossed the box of money on the couch. A few bills flew into the air and fluttered to the floor. She stood staring at them. "He was such a good boy before his mother died. He was only ten, too young to be without his mama."

"She was your sister, wasn't she?" Hannah put an arm around her shoulder.

"Yes. We all suffered when she went, but Tom most of all. If only he'd moved in with us then I could have raised him along with my own four and he would have turned out different."

"I'm sure you're right," Nancy said. "Why didn't he come to live with you?"

"His father wouldn't let him. Jack was a selfish man—never thought of what was best for the boy. Kept him out of school half the time to work his fishing boat. All Jack saw when he looked at Tom was an extra hand to do the work. And he drove the boy hard."

"But how could he take him out of school?" Nancy asked. "That's against the law."

Sarah sighed and sank down into a rocking chair. "You don't know Islanders. Fishing was our life, until the fish disappeared. All those foreign trawlers and factory ships just destroyed the fishing grounds. Most men turned to other work, but some—Jack included—wouldn't give up the sea, even when it didn't pay to go out."

"D.J. said Tom loved boats," Nancy commented.

"He did. He was a lonesome boy. Except for D.J., he didn't bother with friends. Boats were his life. After the sea took Jack, Tom was always looking for a spot on someone's crew. He'd do the meanest job, just to be on the water."

"What happened to his father?" Hannah asked.

"Jack was out alone, setting a seining net. Got

his leg tangled in a line and was dragged over and down. The boat drifted until it was wrecked on Black Rock Point, so Tom lost both it and his father. I'm not sure which he minded more."

Nancy was stunned by Sarah's last statement. Not quite sure what to say, she decided to take action. "I'd better phone the police."

Hannah nodded at Nancy. She, too, seemed shocked. "Come out to the kitchen with me, Sarah. We'll make a nice pot of tea."

Nancy called the station. In about ten minutes Hathaway arrived to collect the money and take Sarah's statement. He told Nancy they still hadn't found Hank, the construction worker who had hit her moped, but he was sure he'd be picked up soon.

After he left, Nancy helped Hannah fix a supper of omelets for the three of them. Afterward, Sarah let Hannah help her up to bed.

The rain had started by the time Nancy and Hannah left and it was a wet, miserable ride home.

As soon as they got back to the cottage, Nancy tried to phone Barb. There was no answer. She shrugged. Her curiosity about Angie and Scott's relationship was overshadowed by Sarah's discovery and the questions it raised about the murder case.

She took a long hot shower and went to bed. As she closed her eyes she pictured the boxful of money. D.J. must know how Tom got so much cash, she thought, and he's going to have to tell me.

Nancy awoke to rain drumming loudly on the roof and wind shrieking around the house. Hannah made blueberry pancakes and the two of them sat in the cozy kitchen, watching the branches of a willow tree beat against the window.

"All that money," Hannah said, shaking her head. "I couldn't get it out of my mind last night."

"I know what you mean." Nancy took a sip of coffee. "I'm sure the money is the key to why Tom was murdered. When I examined D.J.'s books, it was clear he makes a good profit in his business. He'd be able to pay Tom for whatever he was doing, but I don't see him murdering his best friend, unless it was a fight that got out of hand."

"Both those boys were hot tempered, from what you've told me," Hannah said. "And if they were in love with the same girl . . ."

"I know, it makes sense," Nancy agreed. "With D.J.'s hammer found at the murder scene, it seems like the police have a good case. But there's someone else I'm considering as a suspect."

"Who?" Hannah asked.

"Scott Winchester." Nancy told her about the visit to the yacht the day before. "So, there are several reasons why he looks suspicious. He has money to pay Tom. He has a bruise on his face, and we know Tom was in a fight. And apparently he's the last person to be seen with Tom before he was killed. But most important, I'm sure he was hiding something when I asked him about the murder."

"Still, why would he kill Tom?" Hannah asked. "You always say look for the motive."

"I don't know the answer to that yet," Nancy replied. "But I'm going to find out."

"Maybe it's connected to this strange business with Angie," Hannah said. "But she's such a sweet girl, I'd hate to think she's involved in this."

"I feel the same way." Nancy put down her cup and stood up. "The first thing to do is talk with D.J., then I'll question Scott again."

"I wish you wouldn't go out in this storm," Hannah said. "This weather could drown a duck."

"I have to talk to D.J. in person. I know he won't tell me anything over the phone." Nancy put on her slicker.

"It isn't safe out there. Just look how that wind is blowing!" Hannah pointed at the window.

"I'll be careful," Nancy promised. "And I'll be back soon—I'm not going far."

She saw little traffic as she rode toward D.J.'s barn off West Side Road. The streets were slick, and the gusty wind threatened to blow her moped off the road. The storm was rapidly turning into a gale.

When she reached the barn, she was surprised to see that D.J. wasn't home. The only other place she could think to look for him was at the construction site. He might have gone out to check on the house and the tarps they had tied on. Driving slowly, she made it safely out to the Winchester place. The isolated, half-finished house was ominous on such a bleak day.

At first glance she thought the site was deserted, but then she spotted deep tire tracks in the mud. Taking a closer look, she realized they hadn't been made long before. She followed the tracks and found a pickup truck parked behind the house.

Nancy got off her moped and found a spot where she could slip under the blue plastic tarp that covered the house. She stepped into a large empty room. The light that filtered through the blue-covered windows was eerie, and the wind whistled in every crack and corner.

"Hello," she called. "Anyone here?"

Heavy footsteps sounded overhead. "Who is it?" a deep voice said.

"It's Nancy Drew. Is that you, D.J.?"

"Stay there. I'm coming." The footsteps thudded across the ceiling, then down the raw wood staircase at the end of the room. Gradually D.J. Divott came into view. "What do you want?" he asked rudely.

"We need to talk, D.J." Nancy's heart beat a little faster as the huge, scowling man approached her. In spite of her resolve, a thought popped into her mind—this is a man who is suspected of murder, and I'm all alone with him. She took a deep breath. "D.J., please listen to me. I know you were a good friend of Tom, and I respect you for wanting to keep his secret—"

"Are you playing Little Miss Detective again?" He sneered. "I told you before—*give it up.* Tom was my buddy and I'm not ratting on him!"

Nancy thought a moment. D.J. was one stubborn, stiff-necked Yankee, as Barb had said. She had to find a way to break through his misguided loyalty to his dead friend. D.J. was strong and tough. Nancy decided to play by his rules. She would be strong and tough, too. The tactic might backfire, but she'd give it a try.

"Did you murder Tom Haines?" she asked flatly.

"No!" D.J. bellowed, his voice echoing in the empty room.

Nancy refused to be intimidated. "Then why was your hammer found near the grave?"

"I already told the police! Why doesn't anyone believe me? I lent that hammer to Tom months ago! He must have taken it with him, thinking he was walking into a trap." D.J.'s voice turned bitter. "And he did."

Nancy folded her arms across her chest. "I'm almost sure that the person who killed him is the same one who was paying Tom all that money he was flashing around. Don't you understand? If you don't talk, you could be protecting the murderer."

D.J. laughed. "I know who the murderer is!"

"You do?"

"Sure, and I told the police, too. He was the last person to see Tom alive and they know it. Of course they won't do anything about it, not with a rich, powerful daddy protecting the little wimp."

"You mean—"

"You'd better believe it!" D.J. shouted. "Scott Winchester killed my best friend!"

Chapter

Ten

WHY ARE YOU SO SURE Scott murdered Tom?"
Nancy asked. She shivered in her damp clothes in
the empty, cold room.

D.J. scowled. "Lots of reasons. I saw them
together Friday night, leaving the Spotted Dog
about nine o'clock. They didn't notice me—I
was in the pickup and it was dark. They rode off,
Tom following Scott, and that was it. I never saw
Tom again."

Under D.J.'s anger and bitterness, Nancy
heard despair. She remembered Barb's words—
"Inside he's really hurting." She spoke quietly.
"That's not conclusive evidence."

"That's what the police said." D.J. rubbed his
chest as if it ached. "They even suggested I was
making it up to throw suspicion off myself."

"Were you?" The same thought had occurred to Nancy.

"No!" D.J. picked up a chunk of scrap wood and threw it across the room. "Why doesn't anyone believe me! I know Scott did it!"

"But why would he?" Nancy said.

"Because he was blackmailing Scott!" D.J. groaned as soon as he realized he'd blurted out Tom's secret.

Blackmail, Nancy thought. So that's how Tom got so much money.

Suddenly D.J. grabbed Nancy by the shoulders. "Promise you won't tell anyone! You've got to promise!"

His powerful fingers dug into Nancy's flesh. "Let go of me!" she demanded.

"Promise!"

He towered over her, his eyes begging her. Nancy was moved by his pain at betraying his friend.

"All right," she said calmly. "I won't tell anyone without your permission."

D.J. let her go so suddenly that she staggered backward. He stalked across the room, stopped at an empty window frame and stared out, as if he were looking at a view instead of a blue plastic tarp.

For a moment neither of them said anything.

Finally D.J. turned to her. "I'm sorry if I hurt you."

"It's okay. You were upset. When did Tom tell you he was blackmailing Scott?"

"He didn't, exactly." D.J. began to pace. "One night about three weeks ago, I got mad and made him tell me where he was getting all his cash. He admitted it was blackmail, but he wouldn't say who was paying him. I put two and two together and figured out it was Scott."

"Why Scott?" Nancy leaned against the wall, watching him.

"It's obvious. First, he's rich—he could afford it. No sense squeezing someone who hasn't got it. Second, like I said, they were together the night Tom disappeared."

"Did they hang out together a lot?" Nancy asked.

"No, it was just the opposite." D.J. continued pacing, his boots echoing hollowly in the empty room. "I don't like Mr. Rich Boy, but Tom liked him even less. There had to be a fishy reason for them to be together that night."

"Scott told me it was coincidence," Nancy said. "They just happened to go out at the same time."

D.J. stopped pacing and stared at Nancy. "He's lying. Listen to me—Scott's as jumpy as a frog on a hot stone. He's hiding something, and it's something big—big enough to make him pay Tom to keep his mouth shut."

"But you don't know what he's hiding?"

"No." D.J. slammed his fist into the palm of his other hand. "And there's another reason. The police asked me for the name and address of the guy who ran your moped off the road. I gave it to them, and was glad to. Hank was a troublemaker from his first day on the job. And you know who hired him from the mainland when one of my guys got sick?"

"Scott Winchester," Nancy said.

"You got it." D.J. nodded.

"Have you explained all this to the police?"

"Everything but the blackmail." He shook his head and looked up at the ceiling.

"Tom, you crazy fool! Why did you let yourself get into so much trouble? I tried to help you, you know I did! You stupid jerk!" D.J. covered his face with his hands. His shoulders began to shake.

After a moment Nancy went over and touched his back. D.J. pulled away, as if stung. "Go away. Leave me alone," he muttered.

"I'm sorry, D.J., I really am." Nancy left quietly, wishing she could do more to help him.

It was still pouring, the rain blowing almost sideways. As Nancy slowly rode back to the cottage, she went over D.J.'s reasons for believing Scott was guilty. She had begun to like Scott during their talk on the yacht, but she had to admit the circumstantial evidence was building against him. She had to find out what he was hiding.

Hannah had invited Sarah over for lunch, and after Nancy changed into dry clothes, she helped prepare crab salad and blackberry cobbler. A big pot of clam chowder was simmering on the back of the stove, and the kitchen smelled delicious. While they worked, Nancy filled Hannah in on the latest developments in the case, leaving out the blackmail information, as she'd promised D.J. she would.

"Hmmm," Hannah said, mulling over what Nancy had told her. "Scott says one thing about Friday night, D.J. says another and claims Scott's lying. Which one do you believe, Nancy?"

"I'm not sure yet. I want to question Scott again, but I think it might be a good idea to talk to Angie first. She dated Scott for a long time and she must know him pretty well."

Sarah arrived just then. She looked tired but she cheered up a bit when she passed around the pictures of her latest grandchild. During lunch she and Hannah talked about babies and quilting.

The doorbell rang just as Nancy served the coffee. When she opened the front door, she found Jim Hathaway on the porch, rainwater streaming off his slicker. "Hi," he said. "I thought I'd stop by and give you the latest news—or lack of it."

"Come in," Nancy said. "You're just in time for dessert."

"Thanks, anyway, but I've had lunch." Jim took off his hat and shrugged out of his rain gear.

"Blackberry cobbler?" Nancy said, prodding.

"Well . . . I didn't eat all *that* much." Jim grinned.

Nancy pulled another chair up to the table and gave Jim a huge portion.

Sarah let him enjoy the first few bites before she asked, "Have you been able to find out where that money came from?"

"I'm afraid not," Jim said. "The bills are almost untraceable. They were all used, with assorted serial numbers. We've sent them off for fingerprinting, but it's unlikely much will turn up."

Nancy nodded.

"There's still more bad news, Nancy." Jim took a sip of coffee. "Hank Jenkins, your favorite hit-and-run driver, has disappeared. He never went home after taking the ferry. It seems that he's left town. We've put out bulletins, blanketing the airports and bus stations—but so far, no luck."

"I'm not surprised," Nancy said. "If he abandoned an almost-new motorcycle, he must have been paid plenty to get lost."

"That's what we figure, but don't worry, we'll find him sooner or later." Jim turned to Hannah. "This is the best cobbler I've ever tasted, Ms. Gruen. Did you make it yourself?"

Hannah smiled. "It's an old family recipe."

Nancy had the feeling that he was deliberately changing the subject. "Jim, would you like more coffee?" she asked. "It's in the kitchen."

"I'll come with you." He flashed her a look of gratitude and stood up from the table.

Out in the kitchen, Nancy said, "Do you have more bad news that you didn't want Sarah to hear?"

"Yes." Jim sighed. "We just got the lab results on the hammer you found in the pond. There's no trace of blood, hair, or any other sign that it was the murder weapon. Plus, the coroner says the lethal wound on the skull was caused by an irregular, sharp object larger than a hammer."

"Does that mean D.J. is no longer your main suspect?" Nancy asked.

"Yes, although we haven't ruled him out."

"I wonder how the hammer got in the pond," Nancy mused. "Tom and his killer fought over it and one of them flung it away. I suppose there were no fingerprints on it?"

"Not after several days in the water."

"A large, irregular, sharp object . . ." Nancy tried to picture the scene around the grave—the pond and fields. "The rock wall! Of course!"

"That was my idea, too," Jim said. "One of those stones could inflict a wound like Tom's."

"Now I'm almost sorry I spotted the hammer," Nancy said. "Maybe you'd have checked the wall sooner if you didn't think you'd already found the murder weapon."

"If the murderer was smart, he took it with him. With all the rocks lying around this island, he could have dropped it anywhere and we'd never find it." He shrugged. "I'd better get back to the station."

They returned to the dining room. Jim said to Hannah, "Thank you for the cobbler. It was great."

Nancy walked him to the door. If anything, the storm had grown worse. She could taste salt spray mixed with the rain that blew into her face.

After Jim left, she decided to run over and see if Angie was home. Although Angie and Scott were no longer dating, she could tell Nancy what kind of person he was. She might even know what secret Scott was hiding. Nancy grabbed her yellow slicker.

"*Now* where are you off to?" Hannah asked.

She smiled. "Don't worry, I'm only going around the corner to Barb and Angie's place. I'll be back soon. 'Bye, Sarah, it was good to see you again."

She slipped out the door and into the gale. Her sneakers were soaked in two seconds and her jeans were wringing wet by the time she walked the short distance to the girls' apartment.

When Nancy knocked, Angie opened her door only a crack. "I-I'm sorry, Nancy, Barb's not here and I'm really busy right now."

"Can I come in for just a second? I need to talk

to you. It's important." Nancy shivered as a gust of wind blew back the hood of her slicker and cold rainwater trickled down her neck.

Angie leaned out and peered behind Nancy, checking up and down the street. "Okay, but only a second. I-I'm getting ready for work."

"Thanks." Nancy stepped inside the cheerful apartment and took off her dripping jacket. "I had a long talk with D.J. this morning. He made some strong accusations against the guy you used to date. I'm hoping you can tell me a little bit about Scott—"

"Scott?" Angie squealed. "Scott Winchester?"

"Yes, I know you broke up and I guess it was pretty painful for you, but—"

"I'm not going to tell you anything about him, not a thing!" Angie's face was rigid and pale. "If that's what you came for, please leave right now!"

"Gee, Angie, I'm sorry," Nancy said. "I didn't mean to upset you. I—"

Someone knocked on the door. Angie whirled around and stared at it, frozen.

"Would you like me to answer it?" Nancy asked.

"No! Don't! You have to go!"

"All right, but the only way I can leave is through that door," Nancy pointed out gently.

"Oh no, this is awful! I told him it was too risky! Why did I ever—"

The door opened. "Hey, Angie, what kind of wife keeps her husband waiting in the pouring . . ."

Scott Winchester's voice trailed off as he spotted Nancy. Silently he stepped inside and shut the door behind him.

The silence grew as Nancy turned from Angie to Scott and back again. Finally she said, "Did I hear you correctly?"

Scott walked over to Angie and put his arm around her. "Yes, you did. This is my wife, Angelina Winchester."

Chapter

Eleven

"YOU'RE SECRETLY MARRIED," Nancy stated, amazed.

Her mind raced, absorbing the news. She had come hoping that Angie could give her information about her former boyfriend. Now she realized she'd been about to ask a wife to speak against her husband.

"No one knows about it, Nancy," Angie said. "Please, *please* promise you won't tell anyone."

Scott and Angie seemed to be so much in love, Nancy immediately said, "All right, I promise. But why is it a secret?"

Scott and Angie exchanged glances, then she said, "It's a long story. Why don't I make some hot chocolate and we'll explain."

"That sounds good," Nancy said. "But don't you have to go to work?"

Angie blushed. "That was just an excuse. I wanted you to leave before Scott got here."

Nancy and Scott settled on cushions around the low table while Angie bustled around the tiny kitchenette. Nancy watched her pour milk in a pan and add cocoa. "I assume you faked the breakup so people wouldn't suspect you're actually married."

"Well, sort of." Angie hesitated.

"You don't have to tell me, you know," Nancy said. "I'll still keep my promise."

"To be honest," Scott said, "it will be a relief to talk about it. We're so happy together, every time I open my mouth I want to blurt out the truth."

"You silly . . ." Angie grinned at Scott.

Suddenly something occurred to Nancy. Was this the secret Scott had been hiding? Was Tom blackmailing him because he'd found out he was married? "Why *did* you pretend to break up then?" she asked.

"My father," Scott said bitterly. He tugged at the collar of his sweater as if it were choking him. "He—disapproves of Angie and he'd be furious if he knew we were married. I took Angie home to meet him once. He immediately had her family investigated and decided she didn't come from the 'proper' background."

"But you told me her family was wonderful," Nancy said.

"They are! Hardworking, warm, funny—just

96

great people." Scott gazed at Angie with affection.

"Thanks, *cara mia.*" Angie left the pot on the stove and knelt down to hug him. "But they're immigrants," she told Nancy. "Mama and Papa left Italy when they were teenagers and they speak with an accent." Deep anger crept into her voice. "It doesn't matter to Congressman Walt Winchester that they built their own business from scratch—"

"They're not bluebloods," Scott finished for her. "Walt Winchester's only child—only *son*—has to marry into a 'good' family, definitely one with plenty of money and connections."

"So he can follow in his daddy's footsteps," Angie added sarcastically. "That includes going to law school, and then, of course, getting into politics."

So it was *Walt* Winchester whom Angie was reacting to when she ran out of the restaurant, Nancy realized. She said, "But plenty of kids make their own choices, live their own lives."

"Plenty of *other* kids," Scott said grimly.

"How can your father stop you?" Nancy asked.

"Money!" Angie jumped up to stir the hot chocolate. "Scott's grandmother left him a large trust fund, but Scott doesn't inherit it until he's thirty, unless his father gives special permission. Of course he won't, if he finds out Scott married me."

"And I need that money now, to finish college and get my master's." Scott swallowed hard. "Dad will only pay for my education if I'm willing to follow in his footsteps. How could I do that anyway? His boots are too big to fill." He gave Nancy an ironic smile and waggled his foot. "He wears a thirteen and I only wear a nine."

Nancy smiled at his joke. "But if you want to finish college, why did you drop out?"

"Dad kept pressuring me," Scott said. "I hated pre-law, but I didn't know what I wanted to study. Now, after working on the new house all summer, I know I want to be an architect."

Angie brought three steaming mugs to the table.

"He'll be a great one, too. He has what they call 'the eye.' It's an instinct for what works in design."

Scott touched her cheek. "My number-one fan, rooting section, and fellow artist."

Nancy once again found herself liking Scott and finding it difficult to believe he might be a murderer. She had to remind herself that she'd met more than one charming killer in her career.

"Scott," Nancy began slowly, "you know Barb wants me to find out if the police really have a case against D. J. Divott."

"Please, Nancy," Angie groaned. "Do we have to talk about the murder now?"

"There's a new development," Nancy said, taking a sip of cocoa.

"What?" Scott said, suddenly alert.

"Last night Tom's aunt found a great deal of money hidden in his room."

"Really?" Angie was surprised. Scott only stared at Nancy.

"Yes." Nancy remembered her promise to D.J., so she phrased her words carefully. "I've been trying to figure out how Tom might have come by so much money. In my experience, sometimes one source of a large amount of cash is . . . blackmail."

Nancy watched Scott's reaction carefully. He said nothing, only blinked his clear blue eyes rapidly for a moment.

"You think Tom was blackmailing someone?" Angie said. "I wouldn't be surprised. He wasn't a very . . . nice person."

"You didn't like him?" Nancy asked.

"He was a jerk," Angie said. "A real loud-mouth, always bragging about how good he was with boats—and girls."

"But Barb liked him."

"Barb likes everyone," Angie said. "She grew up in South Boston and knows a hundred guys like Tom. If they give her any sass, she gives it right back, and then some."

Nancy nodded. She'd been watching Scott while talking to Angie and was disturbed by what she saw. Emotion seemed to flicker under his outwardly calm manner. Her mention of blackmail had obviously triggered something—but what?

"Scott, what do you think about my theory?" Nancy asked.

His voice was carefully neutral. "I agree with Angie. Tom wasn't a very nice person."

Nancy realized he wasn't going to reveal any more at that point. "Well, I'd better be going. Hannah's expecting me." She stood up and put on her dripping jacket. "Congratulations, you newlyweds. I'm really happy for you."

Scott and Angie walked her to the door. Nancy went out into the storm and made her way home.

She found that Sarah had left and Hannah was in the living room, listening to music on the radio while she worked on her quilt.

"Hannah," Nancy said, sitting in one of the overstuffed chairs, "I've just been talking to Angie and Scott—"

Hannah's eyebrows went up. "Angie *and* Scott?"

Nancy nodded. "I promised I wouldn't tell, but I don't think they'd mind if you knew. I'm sure you won't mention it to anyone. Angie and Scott are secretly married."

"I can't believe it," Hannah said, putting down her quilting. She thought a moment. "Then why did Angie run out of the restaurant the other night?"

Nancy explained how Walt Winchester felt about Angie, and the fact that the congressman controlled Scott's trust fund. She also told her about D.J.'s assertion that Tom Haines had been blackmailing Scott. "If Tom found out about the secret marriage, it's possible that Scott would have paid him to keep quiet."

Hannah frowned and shook her head.

"And if we assume that Tom was killed by the person he was blackmailing, that means Scott is the murderer," Nancy said.

"That handsome young man?" Hannah said.

"I know. But anyone can be pushed to the breaking point. And dropping out of college shows that Scott doesn't always react well under pressure. If Tom kept asking for more and more money, the way blackmailers often do, Scott might have exploded."

"Killing Tom could have been an accident," Hannah said. "Maybe he didn't mean to do it. The police know there was a fight before Tom received the blow that actually killed him."

"And Scott has a bruise on his cheek," Nancy said. "I'm going to ask him where he got it the next time I see him. Also, D.J. saw Tom and Scott leaving the Spotted Dog together the night Tom died." Nancy sighed. "Poor Angie. It doesn't look good for Scott."

"Don't you need proof, Nancy?" Hannah said. "That's what you always tell me."

"You're absolutely right, Hannah. I need to find a way to search Scott's cabin on the yacht. There might be a clue there."

"But don't forget," Hannah said, "you only have D.J.'s word for it that Scott and Tom were together that night. And D.J.'s still a suspect."

"Good point," Nancy said thoughtfully.

"Just be careful," Hannah said. "Don't take any chances. The police will solve this murder sooner or later."

"In the meantime, though, people like Sarah are suffering. And the killer is walking around free."

The telephone rang and Nancy answered it.

"Isn't it incredible?" Barb sounded so excited Nancy hardly recognized her voice. "Angie told me the news! She said if she could trust you, she could trust her best friend—me, of course—to keep the big secret. Can you believe it? I've been living with a married woman and didn't even know it!"

"You sound happy," Nancy said.

"I am! It's so romantic! And guess what? Scott's father is in New York and won't be able to fly back to the island until this gale blows over, so Scott and Angie have decided to have a little wedding celebration. We're invited to Scott's yacht tonight for a lobster dinner. Can you make it?"

"Sure," Nancy said. "I'd love to." She wondered if she might find an opportunity to search Scott's cabin some time during the evening.

"Great! Scott will pick us up on the dock at seven. If anyone sees us, this will confirm his playboy image for good. One guy entertaining three girls—how the gossips will love it!"

The wind had begun to die down but the rain was still heavy when Scott ferried them out to the yacht. The girls carried dry clothes in plastic bags, knowing they'd be soaked by the time they arrived.

"I'm sorry to drag you out into the harbor on a night like this," Scott said as he helped them up the boarding ladder. "But I can't leave *Emily Sue* alone until this storm's over. I feel guilty enough deserting her this afternoon for a couple of hours."

Angie stepped on deck. "Are you telling me a boat is just as important as your wife?" she said, pretending to be angry.

"Of course not." Scott grinned. "The boat is *more* important."

"Oh, you!" Angie chased him down into the cabin, threatening dire revenge.

Classic rock 'n' roll songs were on the CD player. While Nancy and Barb shucked ears of corn, Angie put together a huge salad and Scott bravely dropped the lobsters in the pot of boiling water.

"Sorry, big fella," he apologized to the last one, "but we all gotta go sometime."

"And someone's gotta do the dirty deed," Angie said, shuddering. "Better you than me."

"Anything for you, my Angelina," Scott said with sudden intensity. "Anything."

Nancy watched him carefully. Did *anything* include murder? she wondered.

Dinner was delicious. Melted butter ran down their chins, the pile of lobster shells grew into a mountain, and Scott won the how-fast-can-you-eat-an-ear-of-corn contest. Everyone groaned when Angie cleared off the table and plunked down three tubs of ice cream and six kinds of toppings.

"I can't eat another bite," Barb said.

"You don't have to eat it," Angie said. "You just have to create it. There's a prize for the most original sundae. Now, here are peanuts, fudge sauce, whipped cream, marshmallows, cherries, olives—"

"Olives!" Barb shrieked. "On ice cream?"

"Why not?" Angie grinned.

"If you'll excuse me a moment," Nancy said, "I think I'll go wash up before I build my version of the Leaning Tower of Pisa. Be right back."

One of the bathrooms was located off Scott's cabin, where the girls had changed into dry clothes earlier. Nancy shut the cabin door, washed her hands, then began to search the room.

Scott's things were all neatly stowed away. She found nothing but clothes in the built-in drawers and books on the shelves. She opened the hanging locker and found shirts, slacks, and jeans. She felt around in the pockets. She found loose change, a tiny pocketknife, some string, and other odds and ends.

When she came to the faded pair of jeans Scott had been wearing the day before, she slid her fingers into the front pocket. There she found the folded piece of paper he had been playing with. She opened it and read.

"Bring twice as much $ as before. Pay up or you know what will happen. Tonite. Same place. 10 P.M."

It was signed, *T*.

Chapter

Twelve

THE BLACKMAIL NOTE shook in Nancy's hand. She had found the proof she was looking for, but she wasn't happy about it. It seemed almost certain that Angie was married to a murderer.

She slipped the note into her pocket, to give to the police later, then had another thought. There was no hard evidence proving that Tom had been murdered by the person he was blackmailing. That was only a theory. She decided to wait and talk to Scott before taking any action.

She returned to the party and tried to join in the spirit of the evening. Angie won the Wicked Sundae contest by creating an erupting volcano, with fudge sauce and cherries for the lava flow. They played a hilarious game of Old Maid, with Scott and Angie cheating like mad, trying to help each other win.

It was late by the time Scott took the girls back to shore. Nancy returned to the cottage and fell into bed, exhausted by her efforts to appear carefree when she knew she might be celebrating the wedding of a killer.

She woke up Thursday morning to find the storm had blown away, leaving the island clean and bright under a clear sky. Nancy hoped the good weather would hold because George and Bess were arriving the next day. She also hoped the case would be solved by then.

After breakfast her father, Carson Drew, called. They chatted for a while before Nancy mentioned the murder investigation.

"Don't tell me you've taken on another case, Nancy," Carson said. "You're supposed to be on vacation."

"I didn't plan to get involved," she said, then explained to him what had happened.

"Winchester . . ." Carson mused. "Seems to me I've heard something about him. I can't remember exactly what, but why don't I check it out?"

"Thanks, Dad," Nancy said. "That would be great."

After Nancy said goodbye, Hannah took the receiver, quizzing him on whether he was eating properly and getting enough rest.

"I know him," she told Nancy after hanging up. "All he's thinking about is that trial. He could eat a sawdust sandwich and claim it was delicious when he's caught up like this. And you're just as bad. You hardly touched your breakfast."

"I ate enough last night to last me for three days, Hannah," Nancy said. "Besides, this case worries me, especially the blackmail note. I know the evidence points to Scott, but I don't feel satisfied. If only the police could track down the guy who ran me off the road, we could find out who paid him to do it. Odds are it was the murderer, trying to stop my investigation. I think I'll call Jim right now."

Jim was busy, but he returned Nancy's call a few minutes later. "Sorry, Nancy," he reported. "We still haven't found Hank yet, but we're tracking down a lead in Vermont. I'll let you know the minute we find him."

"Thanks. Any other news?"

"Yes, we found a notepad in Tom's room with imprints of the last message written in it. Now we know where he got all that money! It was a blackmail note!"

Nancy was relieved she wouldn't have to keep D.J.'s secret any longer. She had felt guilty about withholding evidence, but the police had discovered the truth in spite of her promise. "What did the note say?"

The message Jim read was identical to what was in the note she had found in Scott's pocket. Nancy knew she had to tell Jim about her discovery and give him the note, but she felt she owed it to Scott to discuss it with him first.

"Jim, would you meet me for lunch? I may have some information for you."

"Sure. Give me a call when you're ready."

A short while later Nancy rode over to Great Salt Pond, looking for Scott. The Winchester dinghy, *SueSue,* was tied at the pier and the dock boy said Scott had gone ashore a short while before. Nancy assumed he'd be at the construction site, and headed over there.

When she reached the house, Scott hadn't arrived yet, but D.J. and his crew were removing the blue tarps.

"The glaziers are coming today to install the window glass, and after that we'll finish up the roof so the house will be weatherproof," D.J. explained. He was much friendlier to Nancy after their talk.

"Do you mind if I look around a bit?" Nancy asked. She considered telling D.J. that the police now knew about Tom's blackmail, but decided he'd be better off hearing it from them.

"Just be careful where you step. There are nails all over the place." D.J. went back to directing his crew.

While she waited for Scott, Nancy took the chance to check out the house. It seemed rather big for two people, but she guessed Walt Winchester did a lot of entertaining. The ground floor was spacious, with a large opening off the living room for sliding glass doors leading out to what a worker told her would be a patio. Upstairs were four bedrooms, plus the master suite, which would have sliding doors out to a deck, too.

She was in the kitchen when she saw Walt Winchester's red sports car roar up the driveway. The congressman was in a black mood. Nancy overheard his conversation through the open window frame. He had apparently driven straight to the site from the airport, where he had just landed.

"My plane is having problems," the congressman complained to D.J. "And the mechanic can't say how long it will take to fix."

"I suppose you can't take any chances with an airplane." D.J. was trying to sound sympathetic, but Nancy could tell he was impatient to get back to work.

"I should hire my own mechanic," Mr. Winchester growled. "These Islanders can't tell their knees from their elbows."

D.J. turned red with his contained rage at the insult, but didn't say anything.

"Okay, Divott," Winchester went on. "Let's take a look around. Any damage from the storm?"

Nancy watched the congressman stride off ahead of D.J. It occurred to her that if Scott had gone home and been with his father last Friday night, he couldn't be the murderer, even if he had been Tom's blackmail victim. With any luck, she'd get a chance to ask the congressman.

Nancy found a sunny spot to wait for both Scott and his father under the master suite at the end of the house. She could hear Winchester roaming all over the site, asking questions and directing the workers. The glaziers arrived and began to install the windows, and the sound of hammers rang out.

Finally Nancy spotted the congressman alone. He was heading for a storage shed set back at a distance from the house.

"Congressman," she said, catching up with him. "May I talk to you a minute?"

He was instantly charming. "Why, Ms. Drew, how long have you been here? I didn't see you arrive."

"I've been trying to keep out of the crew's way," she said. "Actually, I was hoping to see Scott this morning. Do you know where he is?"

"No, I expected to find him here."

"May I ask you a question?" Nancy said.

"Certainly."

"Were you on the island last Friday night?"

Winchester frowned. "Why do you ask?"

"I was just wondering," Nancy said casually.

"Let me think—yes, I believe I was," he said slowly.

"Do you remember where your son was that night after about nine?"

"Scott?" He seemed surprised. "I think he was on the yacht with me. What's this all about?"

"Was he on the boat *all evening?*"

Walt narrowed his eyes. "Why are you asking me about Friday?" He snapped his fingers. "That's when that troublemaker, Tom Haines, was killed, isn't it?"

"Yes, but—"

"Are you implying that you suspect my son?" Winchester said, furious. "He had nothing to do with it! He was on the *Emily Sue* with me and I'll swear to it in a court of law!"

"I'm sorry, Mr. Winchester, I didn't mean to upset you," Nancy said. "If Scott was with you, then obviously he's not guilty of any crime."

Winchester took a deep breath and managed to smile. "Please forgive me for losing my temper. My son is, well, very important to me."

"I understand," Nancy said sympathetically.

"If you'll excuse me," he said politely. "I need to check on the supplies."

"Sure." Nancy watched him go into the storage shed, trying to decide on her next course of action. She considered riding down to the harbor to see if Scott had returned to the yacht, but decided to wait a little longer. She went back to her spot under the far wall of the master suite and sat down on a board.

The warm sun felt good. She leaned back, lifting her face to it, and closed her eyes. I've been on Block Island since Sunday, she thought, and I haven't had a chance to relax on the beach yet—

She heard a slight screeching sound, as if something heavy were being dragged over wood.

Opening her eyes, she raised them. Above her, on the second floor, a set of sliding glass doors was leaning out of the opening cut for them in the wall.

Suddenly the huge panels began to fall—and Nancy was sitting directly under them!

Chapter

Thirteen

NANCY THREW HERSELF to the right and rolled, covering her head and face with her arms.

A split second later she heard a deafening crash.

She raised her head and stared. The heavy glass panels had shattered into a million pieces, broken by the rocks and construction debris lying on the ground near where she had been sitting.

"Nancy, are you all right?" D.J. came around the corner of the house at a run.

"Yes," she said, sitting up. The metal frame that had surrounded the glass lay only inches beyond her feet, bent and twisted.

D.J. knelt beside her. "Are you sure you're okay? What happened?"

"I saw the doors falling and got out of the way just in time." Nancy wiped mud off her cheek.

"Careful, you're covered with splinters." He pulled a sliver of wood from her hair. "How in the world did that thing fall?"

The construction crew arrived, one after another, exclaiming over the accident. Fortunately, Nancy's jeans had provided some protection, although she had a small cut on her arm.

Walt Winchester pushed through the crowd. "I heard a crash. What happened?"

D.J. pointed to the ground. "The sliding doors fell out through the opening on the second floor. Nancy got out of the way just in time."

"Are you all right, Ms. Drew?" Winchester asked.

"I'm fine, just a bit muddy," Nancy said.

Winchester asked, "Who left those doors in such a precarious position?"

The men glanced at one another and shook their heads.

"I want a report from every one of you," the congressman went on. "I want to know where you were and what you were doing before this happened. Follow me."

Nancy watched him lead the construction crew away. D.J. stayed behind. She said to him, "I'm not so sure this was an accident."

D.J. squinted up at the master suite. "You could be right. The opening for the doors is cut to fit them. In order for them to fall through, the frame had to be tipped at an angle. None of my men would be dumb enough to do that."

"Are you sure?" Nancy asked.

D.J. nodded. "I know all these guys. Of course, I don't know the two glaziers. They came over from the mainland."

"Who hired them?"

"Scott. Who else?"

Nancy frowned. She'd been thinking that the fact that Scott wasn't on the site eliminated him as a suspect. Now she realized he could have paid one of the men to attack her, as Hank had been paid.

She walked toward her moped.

"Where are you going?" D.J. asked.

"I've got to find Scott Winchester." Nancy started the motor and rode down the driveway.

Finding Scott wasn't easy. He hadn't returned to the yacht and no one was home at Angie's apartment. Nancy rode to the Bell Buoy and asked one of the waitresses to check the schedule.

"Angie's not due in until the dinner shift," the girl said. "But I saw her a while ago picking up a picnic lunch from the kitchen. You might try Mohegan Bluffs. That's her favorite spot on the island."

Nancy once more climbed on her moped and headed down Spring Street. When she reached the bluffs, she rode past the lighthouse until she found the dirt lane Barb had shown her. She found Angie and Scott on a narrow spit of land overlooking the ocean. She couldn't wait any longer to get Scott alone. She'd have to question him in front of Angie.

They were facing out to sea and didn't notice her on the path behind them. She studied the young couple for a moment. Their picnic basket and blanket were at the very edge of the cliff, and their arms were around each other. They were talking softly and seemed to be very much in love.

Finally she spoke. "Hi."

"Nancy!" Angie said. Both she and Scott jumped in surprise and scrambled to their feet. "What are you doing here?"

Nancy tried to smile. "I'm afraid I'm looking for Scott."

"Me? Why? Is there a problem?" Scott asked. He didn't seem particularly happy to see her, but it could have been because she'd interrupted his time alone with Angie, Nancy told herself.

"There was an accident at the construction site this morning." Nancy told him what had happened.

"I was wondering what happened to you," Angie said. "You're covered with dirt."

Nancy idly brushed off a clump of dried mud clinging to her jeans. "Scott, how well do you know the glaziers you hired to install the window glass?"

"Not at all," he said. "I found their names in the phone book. Are you sure you're not hurt?"

"I'm fine, but I need to ask you another question. How did you get that bruise on your cheek?"

Slightly embarrassed, he touched the bluish yellow spot. "The yacht gibed unexpectedly when I was out sailing and I didn't duck the boom fast enough. Why?"

Nancy didn't answer him. "I've asked you this before, but I have to ask again. How well did you know Tom Haines?"

Scott frowned. "I told you, he was just one of the guys on the crew."

"Did you like him? Did he like you?"

"I think he resented me, to tell you the truth—my father's money, especially. I overheard him calling me Little Rich Boy a couple of times."

Nancy sighed. "I found evidence that indicates you and Tom had another type of relationship."

Scott's face paled. He acted agitated, and almost frightened. "What evidence are you talking about?"

"I found the blackmail note Tom sent you," Nancy said quietly.

"What?" Scott threw his arms out, apparently frustrated. "You've got it all wrong!"

"Scott, take it easy," Angie said.

"Angie—" He turned toward her and his arm hit her chest.

Angie stumbled, then screamed as her foot slid over the edge of the cliff. Scott grabbed her arm, but her weight pulled him to the very edge of the cliff.

Nancy leapt forward and caught Scott by his belt. "I've got you!"

Angie hung over the steep drop, while Scott teetered on the edge, clutching her arm desperately. Only Nancy's strength kept him from being dragged over the side after Angie. Digging her feet into the ground, Nancy threw her weight backward, trying to pull them toward her.

"Hold on, Scott, hold on!" she gasped as she leaned back farther. Slowly Scott inched toward her.

Transferring her weight, Nancy managed to take a step backward, then another. She tightened her grip on Scott's belt and suddenly threw herself flat onto her back. Scott flew toward her, pulling Angie with him.

The three of them sprawled on the grass in a heap. They lay still, panting, their hearts racing.

After a moment Scott groaned and pulled Angie to him, holding her close. "I don't believe it! I almost killed you!"

"It was an accident," Angie said, caressing his cheek.

"It was stupid, stupid, *stupid!*" Scott buried his face in her hair.

Nancy moved away slightly and knelt on the grass. "It was my fault. I shouldn't have upset you. After all, I don't see how you could have killed Tom, even if he *was* blackmailing you. Your father says you were on the yacht with him last Friday night."

Scott's shoulders slumped forward in defeat. "You don't understand." He took a deep breath, shuddering. "My father can't give me an alibi. He wasn't on the yacht himself."

"What do you mean?" Nancy asked, puzzled.

For a long moment he said nothing. His eyes were dull with pain and he was utterly shaken.

Finally Scott raised his head and stared at Nancy. "That blackmail note wasn't sent to me. It was sent to my *father.*"

Chapter

Fourteen

Nancy stared at Scott. "Your father? Why would Tom blackmail him?"

"My father is a two-faced, lying crook." His voice trembled.

"Why do you say that?" Nancy asked.

"What would you think if you knew your father accepted bribes to change his vote?"

"Are you *sure?*" Nancy asked, standing up.

"I caught him at it during spring break." Scott also stood and faced the sea, his back to the girls. "He didn't know I was in the house one afternoon when he had a little business meeting with one of his so-called friends." He turned to Angie. "I couldn't tell you about it—I was too ashamed of him. I didn't know what to do. . . ."

"Is that the real reason you dropped out of college?" Angie asked softly, going to him.

Scott nodded. "There he was, pushing me to become a lawyer and go into politics, just as he had. Then I discover his vote's for sale to the highest bidder."

"Does he know you found out?" Nancy asked.

"No." He sounded both sad and angry.

Nancy thought a moment. "It seems like Tom Haines discovered the same thing and decided to make some money out of it. But why did you have the blackmail note in your pocket?"

"I found it in Dad's cabin when I was getting some papers he wanted me to bring him. I couldn't believe what I was reading. There were several notes. . . ." His voice trailed away.

"What did you do with them?" Nancy asked.

"I burned them, except for the last one. I held on to it, to convince myself it was real," he said bitterly.

"You probably destroyed important evidence. Do you realize what those notes mean?" Nancy asked.

"*Of course I do!*" Scott faced her, a disturbed look in his eyes. "If Dad followed the instructions in the last one and met Tom that night, he could be—"

"The person who murdered Tom," Nancy finished for him.

Scott covered his face with his hands. Angie put her arm around his waist and leaned her head against his shoulder. No one spoke for a moment.

Finally Nancy said, "Your father wasn't on the yacht the night Tom was killed."

"He"—Scott swallowed hard—"wasn't there when I got back from the Spotted Dog."

"What time was that?" Nancy asked.

"About . . . nine-thirty, I guess."

"And Tom's note said to meet him at ten," Nancy said. "What time did your father get back?"

"After midnight," Scott whispered.

"Scott," Nancy said, shaking her head. "Why haven't you told the police?"

"I didn't know what to do!" Scott broke away from Angie and began to pace back and forth. "Turn my dad in to the police? How could I?"

"Did you mention the notes, or anything else, to your father?" Nancy asked.

"No, I couldn't do that either!"

"You are caught in a terrible situation, Scott," Nancy said with sympathy. "But the police have to know about this. I'm meeting Jim Hathaway for lunch and I plan to give the note to him."

"No!" Scott said. "Please, you can't!"

"You'll have to tell the police where you found the blackmail letters," Nancy said firmly. "This can't go on any longer. Do you think it's fair to D. J. Divott or Tom's aunt?"

"She's right, Scott," Angie said quietly.

Scott took both Angie's hands in his. "I know, but I can't turn against my own father."

"Scott, we'll work it out." Angie hugged him. "Let's go to my apartment and talk about it."

Angie gathered up the picnic basket and blanket. "You don't have to make a decision now. We'll figure out the best thing to do." She led Scott down the path.

Nancy watched them go, wondering if the police would believe her about the distinguished congressman without Scott's testimony.

She knew that the one surviving note, now safely hidden in her bedroom, was not strong enough evidence against Winchester. The police would only have her word that Scott had found it in his father's cabin. Nancy needed positive proof that Winchester was guilty of taking bribes, if not murder.

She remembered her lunch with Hannah at the Captain's Catch. She'd seen the man in the business suit leave a battered briefcase with Winchester. What if it had contained, not important papers, as Walt claimed, but something else? She also remembered the congressman's brief flash of annoyance when she pointed out that his friend had forgotten his briefcase.

If she could find the case and it contained evidence of bribery, she would have much stronger proof to give to the police. Winchester had probably taken it to New York with him, but there was a slim chance it was on board the yacht.

Nancy ran to her moped and headed for the cottage. She needed a lookout if she was going to search the boat. She rode past the construction site and was glad to see Winchester's sports car still parked in the driveway.

She reached the cottage quickly and raced in, calling out, "Hannah!"

The housekeeper came out of the kitchen, wiping her hands. "What's happened?"

"Actually, it's what's *going* to happen," Nancy said with a small smile. "I need your help with something."

"Now what are you up to?" Hannah asked.

"I've got to search the Winchesters' yacht." Nancy quickly told her about Scott's discoveries about his father, then explained her plan.

"You think Congressman Winchester is the murderer?" Hannah said. "I'd be more surprised, except that your father called a little while ago. He said there are rumors that Winchester can be bought for the right price. Apparently, there have been a few too many times he's changed his mind when key issues come up for a vote. Of course, there's no proof that he accepted bribes to do so."

"Maybe we can find some," Nancy said. "Come on, we have to get to the harbor while Winchester's still busy at the construction site."

They raced over to Great Salt Pond on their mopeds. The dinghy, *SueSue,* was tied to the dock. Telling the dock boy they were running an errand for Scott, they climbed in, started the little outboard, and headed out to the yacht.

Once on board the *Emily Sue,* Nancy took her lock pick from her fanny pack and opened the padlock that secured the hatch.

"You're pretty quick with that gizmo," Hannah said admiringly. "Now what do we do?"

"You get to keep watch through the portholes. Let me know if you see Winchester's red sports car arrive in the parking lot." Nancy led her down the steps in the main cabin. "He won't be able to see us from shore if we're inside, but we'll need to make a quick getaway. So, call me the minute you spot his car."

"Can do," Hannah said crisply, taking her place near a porthole.

"I'm going to start from the back and work my way forward," Nancy said. She soon found that the bench seats and bunks covered deep storage lockers. In addition, there were plenty of built-in cabinets holding books, navigation tools, pots and pans, and other necessities.

By the time she reached the forward cabin, she was beginning to think her search would turn up nothing. But then, at the bottom of a locker full of extra sails, she found the briefcase.

"This is it, Hannah!" She ran back to the main cabin and showed it to her. "I remember the jagged gash on the side."

"So do I," Hannah said. "Open it quickly. I think I see a red car—no, it's a sedan, not a sports car."

Nancy picked the lock. "We struck gold!" The

briefcase was almost filled with bundles of cash, bound together by paper bands.

"I'll bet Winchester used some of this money to pay off Hank, the hit-and-run motorcycle rider," Nancy said. "When the congressman heard D.J. say I was a detective that day, he must have decided not to take any chances and scare me off the case."

"He was a fool to think you'd give up so easily," Hannah said.

"Thanks." Nancy smiled. "But one thing is clear—you and I witnessed Walt Winchester accepting this briefcase at the Captain's Table."

"Yes, we did. Should we take it to the police?"

"No, it's better to leave it here," Nancy decided. "Winchester just returned from New York this morning. He's not likely to leave again soon since his plane is grounded. I'll tell Jim what we've found and the police can get a warrant to search the yacht."

Nancy replaced the briefcase and covered it with the sails, leaving the locker just as she'd found it. They double-checked the yacht to make sure nothing was out of place and left, locking the hatch behind them.

When they reached the dock, Hannah breathed a sigh of relief. "Goodness, this breaking-and-entering business is nerve-wracking. I don't know when I've felt so tense. Now what do we do?"

Nancy thought for a moment. She and Hannah

could testify that Winchester had accepted the briefcase in the restaurant. Maybe Angie could talk Scott into admitting that he found the blackmail notes in his father's cabin. But so far, they couldn't prove that Winchester killed Tom Haines.

Nancy knew it was almost impossible to commit a crime like murder without leaving any clues. She'd checked the yacht thoroughly. The only other places to look were the congressman's airplane and the construction site. She didn't think he'd have left anything on a plane that was being repaired, but the construction site was a possibility.

"Let's head back to the cottage," Nancy said. "You need a chance to recover from your life of crime, and I've got to make a call."

They made it home quickly, and without a second's pause Nancy called Jim. He was out investigating a complaint. Jim respected her, but Nancy wasn't sure the other police officers would take her accusations against the congressman seriously. So she left a message, saying she'd call back in half an hour. Maybe by then she could present Jim with solid evidence that Winchester was guilty of murder.

Nancy told Hannah her plan and headed out to the construction site. On the way Winchester's red sports car passed her going toward the harbor. He waved to her and she breathed a sigh of relief that he had not returned when she and Hannah were searching his yacht.

She was thankful, too, that he wouldn't be at the construction site. If he was the murderer, he was almost certainly the person who pushed the sliding glass doors toward her.

The construction workers were just taking a break when she arrived. Most moved over to sit under a shady tree on the edge of the property. D.J. told Nancy he was headed into town to pick up lumber.

Nancy simply said she wanted to look around. She trusted D.J. now, but saw no reason to get him involved.

D.J. was in too much of a hurry to question her motives. "I'll be back in twenty minutes," he said.

She watched D.J.'s pickup roar down the driveway, then decided to start with the storage shed set some distance behind the house. It was one place she hadn't explored earlier.

. The shed was full of tools and supplies—an electric saw, ladders, paneling, tape, joint compound. In addition, the men apparently used it to store extra jackets and foul weather gear. A heap of clothes and boots were piled in one corner.

Nancy sorted through the collection. One large pair of men's pants was especially muddy around the cuffs. Next to them, she noticed a pair of cowboy boots caked with dried mud. The initials

W.W. were worked into the design. She checked the number stamped inside. Size thirteen, as Scott had said when he joked about following in his father's footsteps. They had to belong to the congressman.

She took the boots over to the door where the light was better. Turning one of them upside down, she checked the mud that was wedged between the heel and the sole. Then she stooped and picked up a stick lying on the ground.

Nancy poked at the mud. Several chips flaked off. Now she could see that something was imbedded in the mud. The head and body was glossy black, with brilliant orange spots.

It was a dead burying beetle!

Chapter

Fifteen

A BURYING BEETLE on Winchester's boot!" Nancy whispered. Barb had said that almost all the beetles on the island were found at the Lewis-Dickens farm. Nancy knew that the person who dug the grave on the nature preserve had destroyed one of the nests. This beetle must be one of the adults that disappeared.

She had to talk to Jim. Nancy ran down to the trailer and snatched up the phone. Jim was still out. "Please tell him to meet me at the Winchester yacht as soon as he can get there. *It's urgent!*"

The dispatcher promised to contact him. Nancy ran to her moped and took off. When she arrived at the dock, she saw that the *Emily Sue* was gone from its mooring. "Oh, no!" she said out loud.

Nancy scanned the harbor but didn't see it. Finally at the very end of a long pier some distance away, she spotted the *Emily Sue*. She jogged along the shoreline to the longer dock, and ran out to the end. The yacht was tied up by the gas pump, taking on fuel. Through the large, square portholes she spotted Walt Winchester inside.

Where was Jim? Nancy wondered, checking back at the road. She thought about waiting for him, but was afraid Winchester might sail off in the yacht before he arrived.

Ashley Hanna and her cousin were just getting out of a sailboat tied up at the dock. "Ashley, just the person I want to see," Nancy said. "Would you do me a big favor? I'm expecting Sergeant Hathaway to arrive any minute. Could you wait by the parking lot and tell him where to find me? I'll be aboard the *Emily Sue*."

"Sure, Nancy," said Ashley. "What's going on?"

"I'll tell you later," Nancy said. "It's very important." Ashley nodded in comprehension and she and her cousin took off down the pier.

The tide was going out and the yacht's deck was a few feet lower than the dock. Nancy walked over to the ladder and called down, "Congress-man Winchester, may I have permission to board?"

He emerged from below. "Why, Ms. Drew, what a surprise. Please, come aboard."

As she climbed onto the *Emily Sue*'s deck, he took her hand in a gentlemanly way. "Beautiful day, isn't it?" Winchester asked, leading her into the cockpit. "I thought I'd take advantage of this breeze and go for a sail."

Now that she was in the harbor, Nancy realized that the wind was much stronger than it appeared on land. She'd become accustomed to Block Island's constant sea breeze, but she guessed that the wind was blowing close to twenty knots.

"It does look like a good day for sailing," Nancy agreed. "I imagine the *Emily Sue* must be pretty fast under these conditions."

"Oh, yes," Winchester said. "She can really kick up a wake. May I offer you something to drink?"

"Thanks, but I can't stay long." She studied him for a moment. He looked strong enough to get the better of a guy like Tom Haines in a fight.

"What's the matter, Ms. Drew? Why are you looking at me that way?" Winchester said.

"I need to ask you something," Nancy said.

"Then come into the cabin where we can be more comfortable." He turned and led the way down.

Nancy glanced up at the dock before she followed him. Still no sign of Jim. She'd have to proceed on her own.

"Have a seat," Winchester said. "Are you sure you don't want a soda?"

She shook her head. "No, thanks. Congressman, you told me that you and your son were both on this boat last Friday night. But Scott told me *you* weren't here that evening."

"He said that?" Winchester sounded startled. "Well—he's wrong!"

"Scott also said that he found a blackmail note signed *T* among the papers in your cabin."

"Why that sneaky little—" He stopped himself, but his forehead began to glisten with perspiration. "He doesn't know what he's talking about. Scott's always been imaginative—constantly making up stories. His teachers complained about it."

"On Monday," Nancy continued, "Hannah and I saw you at the Captain's Catch. A man talked with you for a short time and left a briefcase for you."

"What's wrong with that?" Winchester pulled out a handkerchief and wiped his forehead. "I told you, it contained important papers."

"Then you won't mind if the police examine it?"

"Of course not." He shrugged. "Unfortunately, it's no longer here. I took it back to New York."

Nancy folded her arms. "I have reason to believe the briefcase is still on this yacht, and that it doesn't contain papers, but money."

"How would you know that?"

"I also found a pair of your boots," Nancy

went on, "that prove that you were at the nature preserve, walking—or digging—in mud."

Winchester stood up, looming over Nancy. "Just exactly what are you trying to—"

"Nancy!" a voice called. "Nancy? Are you here? That nice girl said you were here."

It was Hannah.

"Get rid of her," Winchester growled. "Fast." He yanked open a drawer and grabbed a gun.

Nancy stood slowly and crossed over to the companionway, keeping an eye on the weapon. She eased up the steps, one at a time.

"That's far enough," Winchester ordered.

Nancy's head barely cleared the hatch. "Hannah, I'm here, but I can't talk now."

Hannah peered down from the deck. "Why not? Is Scott with you? I've been looking all over—I couldn't wait to tell you the news. The police found the man who ran you off the road."

"Hannah," Nancy said with meaning. "*Scott* Winchester is not with me."

"Oh." Hannah straightened up slowly. "I see. Well, I'll run along then. . . ."

Nancy knew Hannah understood her and would call the police. Unfortunately, the same thing occurred to Winchester.

"Ms. Gruen!" he called, crossing to the bottom of the steps. Nancy felt the gun dig into her side. "Please come down." It was an order, not an invitation.

Hannah glanced toward the dock. Suddenly

she began to wave at someone. "Hi, Harry! Millie, how have you been?" She took a step away.

"Nice try, Ms. Gruen. But it won't work." His voice was steely.

"I-I don't know wh-what you mean," Hannah stammered. "Those are friends of mine—"

"You're bluffing," he said coldly. "I have a gun on Ms. Drew and I won't hesitate to use it. Please come down. *Right now.*"

Nancy saw Hannah's sturdy shoes appear on the steps. If Hannah hadn't come, she'd have tried a judo move on the congressman. Now she couldn't be sure of disabling him without putting Hannah in danger. He'd already killed once— the hit-and-run-driver was sure to testify to that —and had tried to kill again. Nancy knew he'd shoot if he had to. His cover was blown and he had nothing to lose.

"Ms. Drew, please take a seat on the banquette," Winchester ordered.

Keeping her eye on the gun, she moved over to the dining table and sat on the bench.

"Slide over," he ordered.

Slowly Nancy inched along the booth until she was in the center, where the table was between her and the room.

"That's far enough," he said just as Hannah reached the cabin.

Hannah glanced at Nancy and seemed relieved to find her unhurt.

"Sit down, Ms. Gruen, in the swivel chair where I can see you," he said.

Silently and with dignity, Hannah did as he said.

Nancy looked around. There was nothing in reach she could heave at Winchester, and she couldn't tip the table over because it was bolted to the floor. She could see that Winchester was attempting to appear calm, but sweat was pouring down his face. Her only hope was to goad him into doing something stupid.

"Why did you kill Tom?" Nancy asked suddenly.

Winchester seemed startled. He nervously wiped away the sweat that was trickling down into his eyes.

"I'm really curious," she said innocently.

"That no-good bum?" Winchester said. "He was squeezing me dry. I bought him off at first, but he kept raising his demands. Every time we met he asked for more money. He didn't deserve to live!"

"Did you meet him Friday night, planning to kill him?"

"No!" Winchester wiped his face again. "I told him enough was enough. But he insisted on more money and I . . . lost my temper."

"So you fought, and . . ." Nancy waited.

"He had a hammer! I was only defending myself! I got it away from him and threw it."

"Then what happened?" she asked.

"He came at me and I fought back. Somehow his head hit the rock wall—then he stopped moving."

"If it was self-defense," Nancy said softly, "I'm sure a jury—"

"No jury! The press would find out about the bribes! My career would be ruined!"

In spite of Winchester's fury, he managed to keep the gun steady. She had to keep him talking until Jim showed up.

"How did Tom find out you were accepting the bribes?" she asked.

"He was working on the boat, fixing the roller jib, when I had a, uh, visitor. He must have spied on us, listened in through the hatch. He should have kept his nose out of my business!"

"But don't you see, you didn't plan to kill him," Nancy said reasonably. "If you confessed, I'm sure you'd get a light sentence and then—"

"And then what? I'm a politician! I'd never hold office again! I wouldn't even be able to practice law! I'd have nothing!"

The gun wavered slightly and Nancy tensed, wondering if she could throw herself across the table before he could pull the trigger. Out of the corner of her eye she saw Hannah shake her head slightly, signaling no. She realized Hannah was in a better position to jump Winchester, if he could be distracted long enough.

"Why did you pay Hank to run me off the

road?" Nancy pressed. "Was he supposed to kill me?"

Winchester laughed harshly. "No, just give you a good scare—that's what the man putting in the sliding window was supposed to do, too. Of course, I had no idea what an irritating pest you'd turn out to be!"

Nancy realized that Hannah was on the edge of her seat, her eyes fixed on the gun. Could she cover the six feet that separated her from the congressman fast enough to knock it out of his hand?

Winchester suddenly noticed Hannah, too. "That's enough, Ms. Gruen. I know what you're planning and you can forget it. Now I'll tell you what *I'm* planning. My only hope is to get out of this country on the yacht."

"It's a long way to international waters," Nancy said.

"But I'll make it because I have your friend, Ms. Gruen, here." Winchester suddenly strode across the cabin and jerked Hannah to her feet, pressing the gun barrel into the back of her neck.

Hannah gave out a muffled cry.

"Let her go," Nancy said. "Take me instead."

"Oh, you're coming, too, Ms. Drew, at least part of the way. But first, you will do exactly as I say, won't you?"

"Yes," she said, knowing that if she didn't, Hannah would die.

"First, get up on deck."

Gripping Hannah tightly, he followed Nancy, stopping at the foot of the companionway where he could watch her every move.

Under orders, Nancy disconnected the gas hose, started up the motor, and cast off the mooring lines. She kept scanning the dock and parking lot, but there was still no sign of Jim.

"Hurry up," Winchester hissed. "Put the engine in gear and head for the mouth of the harbor."

Nancy did what she was told. The yacht made a graceful turn and soon slid down the narrow passage between the two long stone breakwaters that led out to sea. They cruised right past the Coast Guard station, but the fear in Hannah's eyes kept Nancy from signaling for help.

The ocean swells were heavy, long, and rolling. After a while Winchester ordered, "Head into the wind and raise the main sail."

Nancy removed the canvas cover and winched the huge sail up the mast. When she finished, she realized that Winchester and Hannah had vanished. But then a door slammed shut below, and Winchester came up on deck, the gun leveled at her.

"What did you do with Hannah?" Nancy demanded.

"She's quite comfortable, I assure you." He checked the sails. "Nice work, Ms. Drew. It's a pity I can't hire you as crew. Unfortunately, you've served your purpose and now it's time for you to jump ship."

Nancy glanced at the shore, guessing they were at least a mile out to sea.

"Over you go," he said, pushing her.

Slowly Nancy climbed up on the outer deck, stepping over the lifelines. Winchester stood close behind her.

"Is Hannah all right?" she asked.

"She will be, if no one tries to follow me. If someone does, you'll never see your friend again."

Nancy tried to swallow, but couldn't. Then Winchester swung the gun. It caught her on the side of the head, and she went plummeting into the cold, choppy sea.

Chapter

Sixteen

STUNNED, NANCY PLUNGED down into the blue water. A single thought whirled in her mind—she had to have air.

Instinctively, she began to claw at the water. The icy chill helped bring her to her senses, and her frantic thrashing turned into smooth strokes. She rose higher and the brightness grew, then she burst through to the surface.

She sucked in a great draft of sweet air and let herself go limp so that she was floating on her back. Gradually her heaving chest and racing heart began to slow to a normal rate. Her head ached and her thoughts were hazy, but somehow she knew that it was important to keep still.

It took tremendous willpower to stay relaxed in a dead man's float as images of what had happened on the yacht flooded back into her mind.

Cautiously, she looked around. As she floated on top of a high swell, she saw the stern of the yacht in the distance. She knew Winchester wouldn't be able to spot her any longer. She hoped he thought she was dead. She glanced toward the shore, then resolutely started to swim.

Settling into a steady, rhythmic pace, she gradually drew closer to shore. The exercise washed away the last traces of fuzziness from her mind, and she began making plans.

Eventually she saw a rocky beach just ahead, and standing there, ready to launch a boat, were Jim Hathaway and a couple of Coast Guardsmen.

Nancy waved and increased her speed. Jim splashed out into the water to help her wade ashore.

"Why didn't you wait for me?" he scolded gently. "I came as soon as I could."

Nancy didn't answer. That was the past—what mattered now was the future. Hannah's future.

"The girl and boy told me you were on the yacht, so I knew something was up. I contacted the Coast Guard and met up with them right away," he explained.

"It's Walt Winchester," she said. "He has Hannah." Quickly she told him about the bribery, the blackmail, and the dead beetle on Winchester's boot.

"I'll radio for backups," Jim said. "Don't worry, we'll get him."

"Jim," Nancy said. "We have to be careful. Winchester mustn't know we're after him. I think we can sneak up on him if we fool him into thinking we're fishing."

"My father owns a lobster boat," Jim said. "It's moored over in Old Harbor."

"That's perfect," Nancy said. "It won't look like we're chasing Winchester if we're busy hauling lobster traps when he sees us."

She turned to the Coast Guardsmen standing beside Jim. "Can you get a fix on the yacht with radar and let us know where to intercept it?"

"Sure," the short one with red hair said. "But we'll have to communicate on a special channel. Winchester is sure to have his shortwave radio tuned in to monitor the usual stations."

"Can you arrange it?" Nancy asked.

"No problem, ma'am."

"Then let's go!" she said to Jim.

Twenty minutes later their lobster boat pulled out of Old Harbor and headed south with Jim at the wheel. Both he and Nancy wore hooded foul-weather jackets to conceal their identities.

Nancy kept thinking about Hannah, hoping she was all right. She told herself Winchester wouldn't hurt her as long as Hannah was useful to him as a hostage. She tried to make herself believe it.

The Coast Guard had advised them that the yacht was headed south on a steady course.

144

Fortunately, their lobster boat was much faster than the *Emily Sue*. They'd be in position to intercept it with plenty of time to establish their cover. When Winchester came close enough to spot them, they'd be working the lobster traps. He'd have no reason to be suspicious.

About half a mile south of Black Rock Point, Jim pulled the boat up to a green-and-white lobster buoy, put the engine in neutral, and showed Nancy how to hook the buoy and pull it aboard. Soon the metal trap, which Jim called a pot, emerged from the sea, dripping and full of wriggling creatures. They put on heavy gloves.

"Toss the junk," Jim said, "but leave the keepers in the pot. Men have been killed for stealing someone else's lobsters."

Nancy watched as he removed several spiny crabs and a large whelk from the trap and tossed them into the ocean. They pulled and emptied several traps while they waited for the yacht.

After rebaiting the fourth trap, Nancy watched it disappear under the waves, then anxiously scanned the horizon for the yacht.

"There it is, Jim! That's the *Emily Sue!*" It was headed toward them, all sails spread.

"What a beauty!" Jim whistled in admiration.

Nancy tugged another trap on board as the yacht closed in on them from the north. Since the wind was out of the west, the huge white sails were stretched out beyond the left side of the yacht.

Jim steered the lobster boat until they were east of *Emily Sue*'s course. That would put them at an angle where they would be hidden behind the large sails as they approached. With any luck, Winchester wouldn't spot them until the last second.

When they judged they were in the right position, Jim throttled back the engine to neutral and Nancy sorted the contents of the trap while they allowed the yacht to close the gap between them. She knew Winchester would assume he'd pass them about fifty yards away if they stayed in place—as he was likely to expect them to do.

The timing had to be perfect. As soon as Nancy was sure the yacht's sails blocked them from Winchester's line of vision, she ran to the forward deck and picked up a line tied to the bow.

She quickly double-checked the noose she had knotted at the end of the line. Satisfied, she signaled Jim at the wheel.

Jim gunned the engine and the lobster boat leapt forward. As soon as the bow was clear of the *Emily Sue*'s sails, Nancy spotted Winchester standing at the wheel. He seemed surprised by their close approach, but didn't recognize her in the slicker.

Seconds later the lobster boat swept past *Emily Sue*'s stern. Nancy tossed the line and the noose landed, slipping over the radar post at the rear of the yacht.

Then she braced herself for the jolt. When the

line tightened, the forward momentum of the lobster boat yanked the stern of the yacht in its direction. The sails flapped wildly as the wind was dumped out of them and the boom swung over the cockpit.

Winchester was thrown off balance by the sudden jerk. He staggered, then saw the boom swinging toward him. He tried to duck and tripped. The boom just missed his head as he fell to the deck.

Jim gunned the engine and swung the lobster boat around until it was aimed at *Emily Sue*'s stern.

Seconds later the bow of the lobster boat crossed behind the yacht. Nancy jumped from its deck into the yacht's cockpit.

Winchester was on his knees, partly tangled in the lines dangling from the mainsail. "You're supposed to be dead!" he screamed when he recognized Nancy.

"Not quite," she said grimly.

"I'll get you yet." Winchester lunged at her.

Nancy neatly stepped aside and gave him a quick karate chop on the neck. Winchester dropped to the deck, motionless. Before he could recover, Nancy grabbed a loose rope and tied his hands behind his back, then bound up his ankles.

Confident that Jim would now radio for the backup boats that had been keeping out of sight, she ran down into the main cabin.

"Hannah! Where are you?" Nancy shouted.

Silence. Winchester wouldn't have already— no, it was unthinkable.

"Hannah! Hannah!" Nancy raced down the hall, flinging open cabin doors.

She heard a faint thump, then another. Finally a weak wail. Following the sounds, she found Hannah in a tiny cabin, tied and gagged.

In a flash she ripped out the gag, then set to work undoing the knots that bound her.

Hannah swallowed several times to wet her dry mouth. Finally she was able to say, "I knew you'd come, Nan dear. But what took you so long?"

The next morning Nancy and her friends gathered in the sunshine on the dock, waiting for the ferry that was bringing George and Bess to the island. Sarah and Hannah stood together, while Nancy talked to Barb, D.J., and Jim.

"How is Scott doing?" Nancy asked.

"Okay, I guess, but it wasn't easy for him to see his father under arrest," Barb said.

"When we brought Winchester into the station," Jim said, "Scott was there. I got the feeling that even though he was upset, he was a bit relieved, too. The last months must have been a nightmare for him."

"Thank goodness he has Angie," Barb said, "and her family. When she called her mom and dad and told them about everything, they insisted that she bring Scott home."

"Here they come now," Jim said.

Scott and Angie, carrying their luggage, walked toward the group on the pier. Scott had dark circles under his eyes and his face was drawn, but Angie squeezed his hand and he managed a weak smile.

"What a send-off committee," Angie said.

Barb grinned. "It's also a welcoming committee, you know. People go, people come. That's the way it is, all summer long on Block."

"We'll be back in a couple of weeks," Angie said.

"Whenever," Barb replied. "Just have a good time and relax."

"Divott." Scott turned to D.J. "I don't know what's going to happen with the house—"

D.J. shrugged. "I'll keep building until someone tells me to stop."

"Thanks." Scott turned to Nancy. "I guess I should thank you, too, even though—"

"Don't worry, I understand." Nancy thought about the crimes Winchester had committed after killing Tom. He might have received a light sentence if he had stopped there. He could have proved self-defense. But attempted murder and kidnapping in addition painted a bleak future for the congressman.

"Here comes the ferry!" Hannah announced.

Nancy watched the big boat pull into the harbor. George and Bess were in the bow, waving madly. Their familiar faces made Nancy feel suddenly happy.

Scott and Angie said goodbye and joined the line waiting to board. The ferry docked, and passengers began pouring off, chattering gaily.

George and Bess rushed over to Nancy and Hannah, full of enthusiasm and hugs. Nancy introduced them to her island friends.

"How's your vacation been going?" George asked, slinging her duffel bag over her shoulder.

"Were you bored?" Bess said, giggling. "I'll bet you missed the excitement of solving crimes."

Hannah winked at Nancy.

"No," Nancy said, grinning. "I didn't miss it. In fact, Block Island is the perfect place to get away from it all. . . ."

Nancy's next case:

A few days at Emerson College is just what Nancy needs. After a long summer of travel, she has a lot of catching up to do with Ned Nickerson. But their sweet reunion suddenly takes a very sour turn. A scandal has erupted on campus, and Nancy's forced to ask some painful questions—questions that could ultimately lead to Ned's expulsion from college!

Never has Nancy faced a more painful investigation. Will it turn Ned against her? Will it destroy her weekend roommate's budding romance with another prime suspect? Breaking the case may break hearts—even her own—but Nancy can't afford *not* to take the risk, for lurking behind the scandal is a secret passion . . . fast turning into a dangerous obsession . . . in *The Cheating Heart,* Case #99 in The Nancy Drew Files™.

THE HARDY BOYS® CASE FILES

Simon & Schuster Mail Order
200 Old Tappan Rd., Old Tappan, N.J. 07675
Please send me the books I have checked above. I am enclosing $_____ (please add $0.75 to cover the postage and handling for each order. Please add appropriate sales tax). Send check or money order—no cash or C.O.D.'s please. Allow up to six weeks for delivery. For purchase over $10.00 you may use VISA: card number, expiration date and customer signature must be included.

Name _____

Address _____

City _____ State/Zip _____

VISA Card # _____ Exp.Date _____

Signature _____ 762-14